MALCOLM'S MARTIANS: EXPLORING MARS

Lost on Mars: Getting Back to Basecamp

by Jason M. Burns

illustrated by Dustin Evans

TORCH GRAPHIC PRESS

Published in the United States of America by Cherry Lake Publishing Group
Ann Arbor, Michigan
www.cherrylakepublishing.com

Reading Adviser: Beth Walker Gambro, MS, Ed., Reading Consultant, Yorkville, IL

Book Designer: Book Buddy Media

Torch Graphic Press is an imprint of Cherry Lake Publishing Group.

Library of Congress Cataloging-in-Publication Data has been filed and is available at catalog.loc.gov

Cherry Lake Publishing Group would like to acknowledge the work of the Partnership for 21st Century
Learning, a Network of Battelle for Kids. Please visit http://www.battelleforkids.org/networks/p21 for
more information.

Printed in the United States of America
Corporate Graphics

TABLE OF CONTENTS

Mission log: July 27, 2055.

Today we are traveling across Mars to see the **yardangs**. I don't know much about these strange rocks yet, but I'm sure Dad will teach my friend Daniela and me all about them. We have to travel really far from camp to get there, but thankfully we have a cool cruiser to drive in. I'm excited to draw the Martians that might have lived in this area of the planet. I wonder what will inspire my creations?

—Malcolm Thomas

yardangs: ridges formed by wind erosion

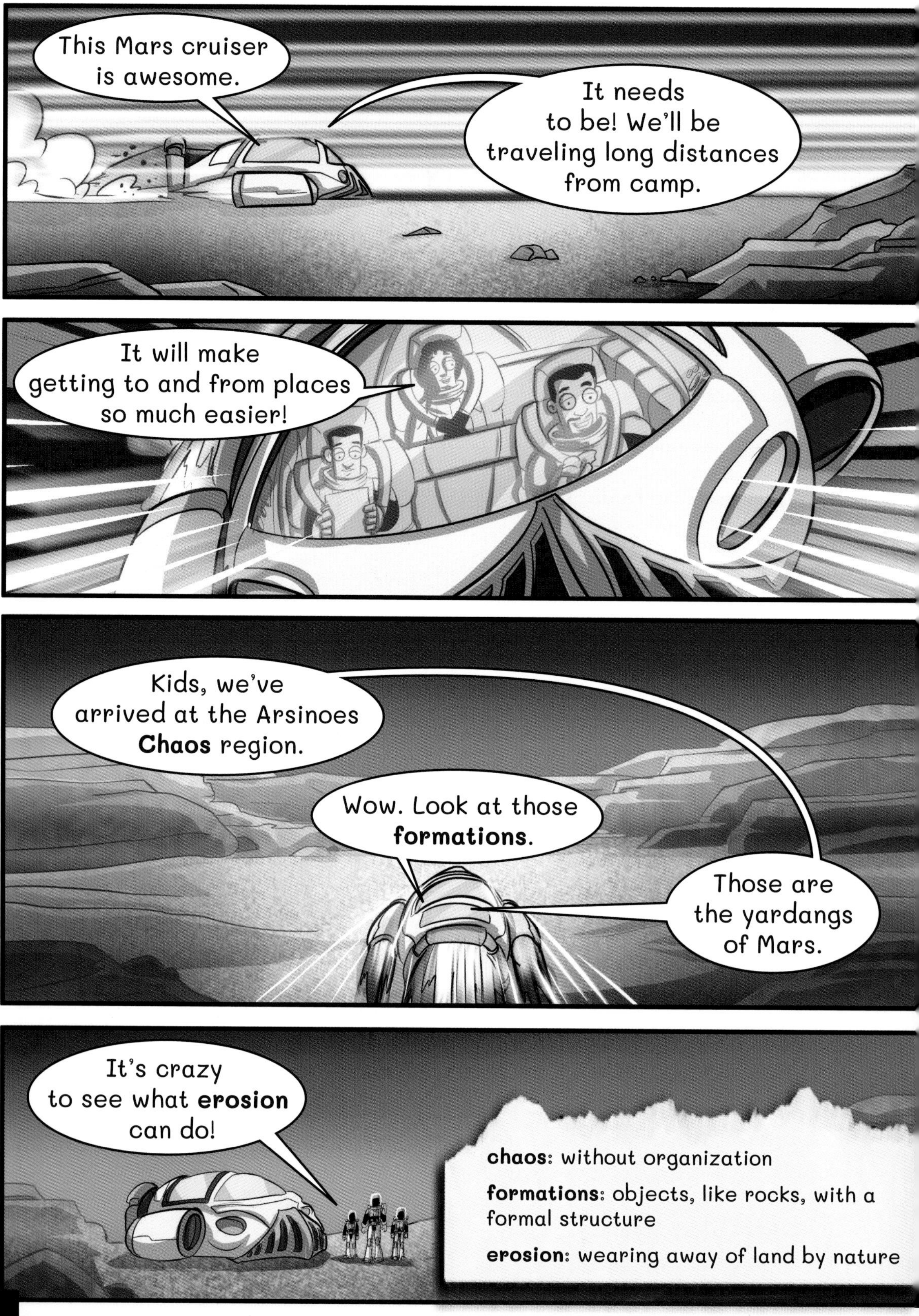
This Mars cruiser is awesome.
It needs to be! We'll be traveling long distances from camp.
It will make getting to and from places so much easier!
Kids, we've arrived at the Arsinoes **Chaos** region.
Wow. Look at those **formations**.
Those are the yardangs of Mars.
It's crazy to see what **erosion** can do!

chaos: without organization

formations: objects, like rocks, with a formal structure

erosion: wearing away of land by nature

THE CASE FOR SPACE

Although Mars has long been characterized by its **craters**, the landscape is quite diverse. Here are some facts about the Arsinoes Chaos region.

•The Arsinoes Chaos region is located in the Valles Marineris **canyon** system, or Mariner Valley.

•Mariner Valley runs along the **equator** of Mars.

•It is as long as the United States.

•It can be as deep as 4 miles (7 kilometers) in some places.

•The Arsinoes Chaos region is in the eastern part of the system.

•Scientists believe the chaotic terrain was created by flowing water in ancient times.

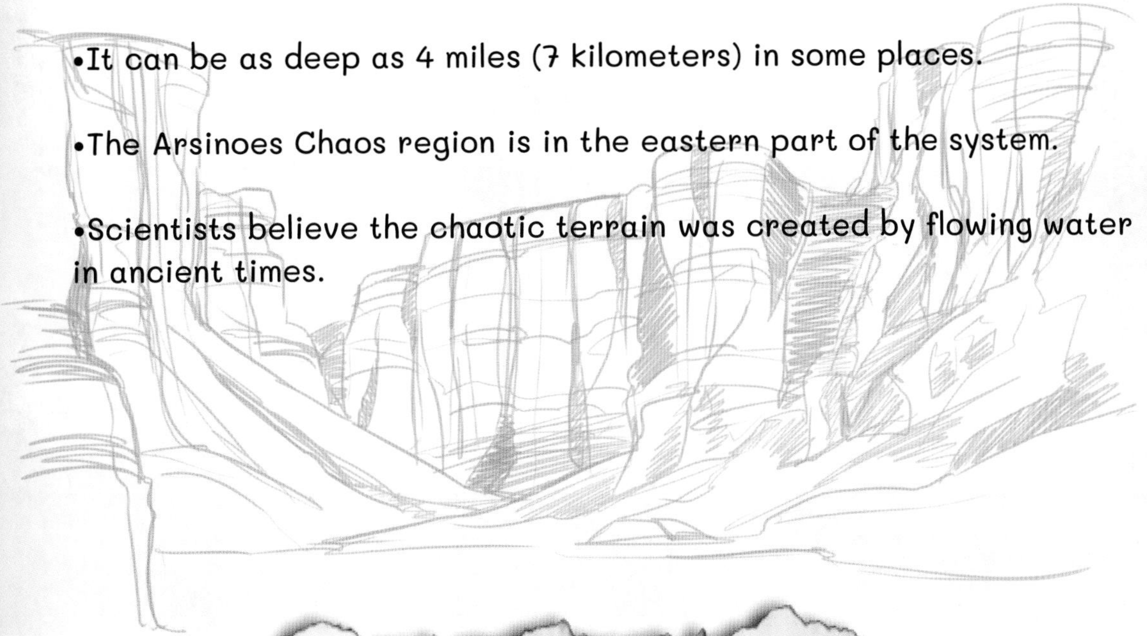

craters: circular depressions in the ground

canyon: a deep valley formed by flowing water

equator: an imaginary line drawn around the middle of a planet that divides it in half

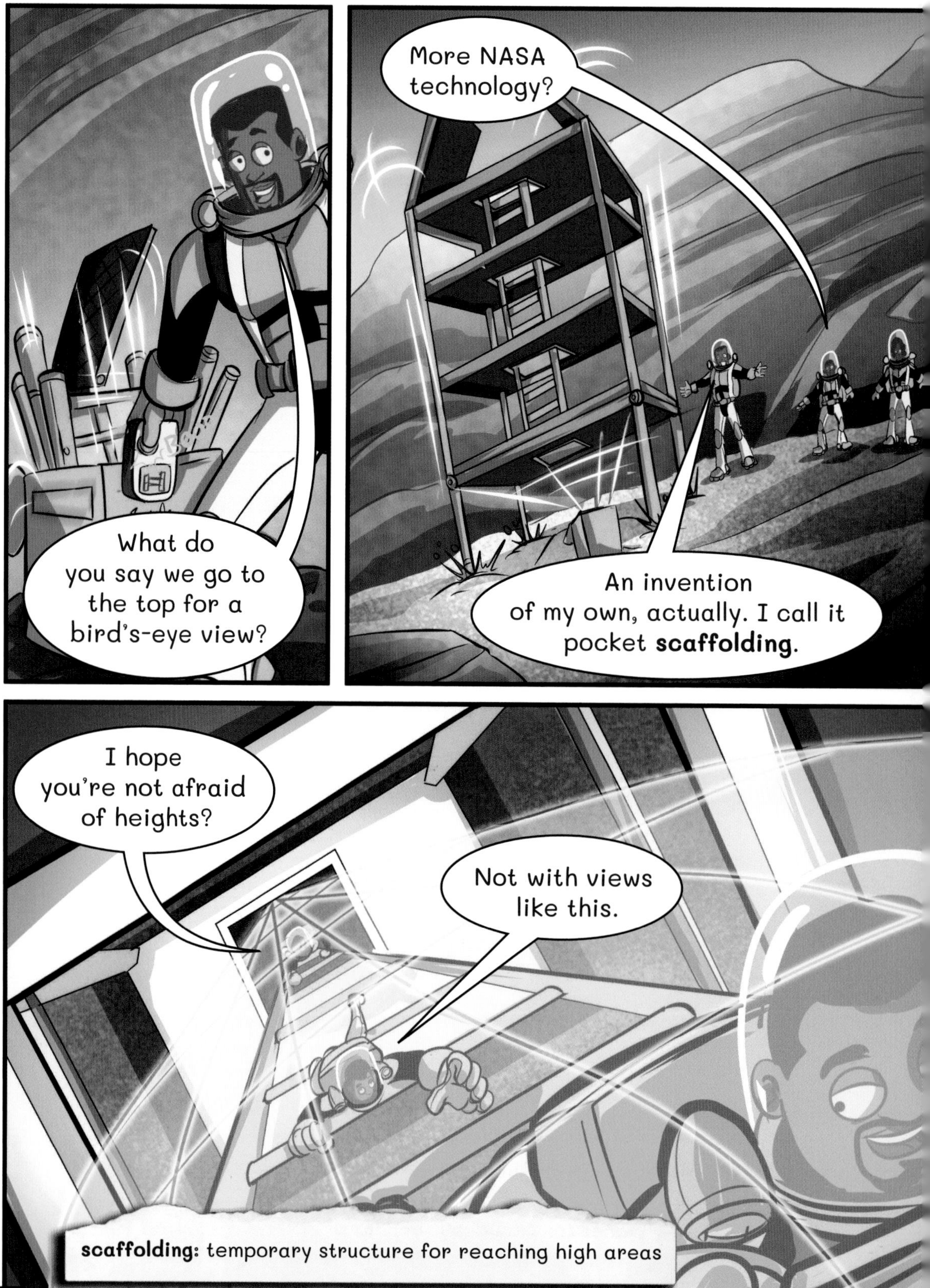
What do you say we go to the top for a bird's-eye view?
More NASA technology?
An invention of my own, actually. I call it pocket **scaffolding**.
I hope you're not afraid of heights?
Not with views like this.
scaffolding: temporary structure for reaching high areas

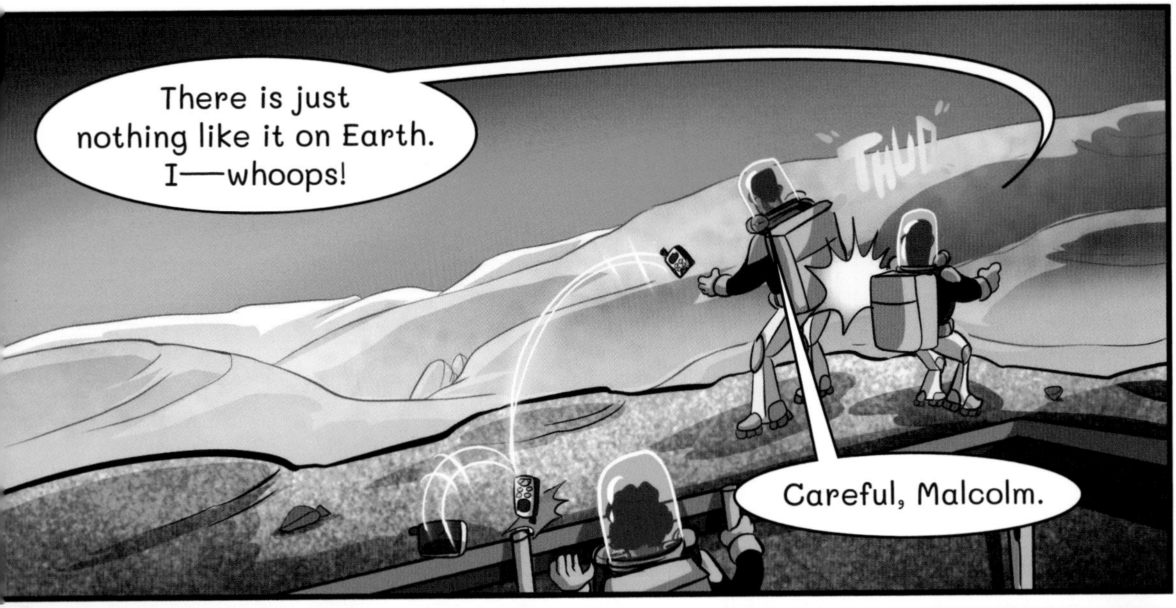
There is just nothing like it on Earth. I—whoops!
THUD
Careful, Malcolm.

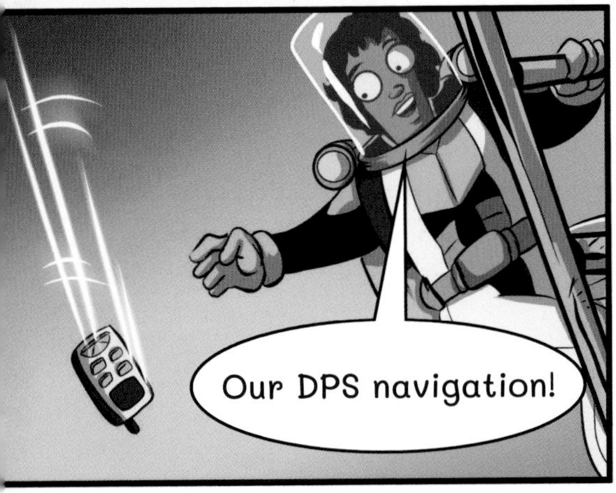
Our DPS navigation!

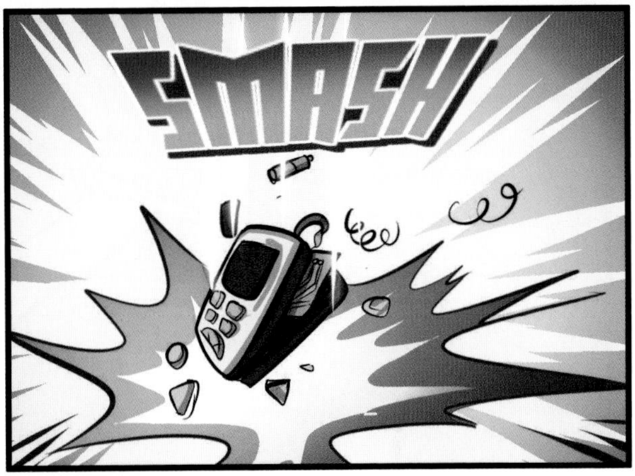
SMASH

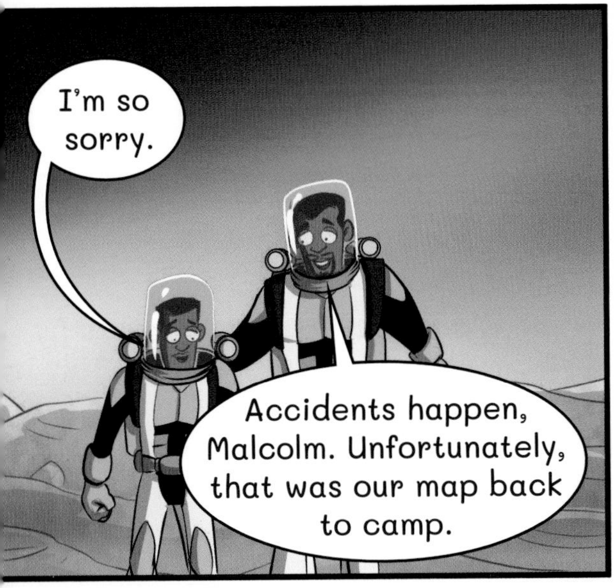
I'm so sorry.
Accidents happen, Malcolm. Unfortunately, that was our map back to camp.

MARS FACT

You can see Mars with your own eyes by simply looking up! Mars moves around in our sky. Books or apps will help you find the best time and place to locate Mars, as well as other stars and planets. Mars will look like a yellow-orange star.

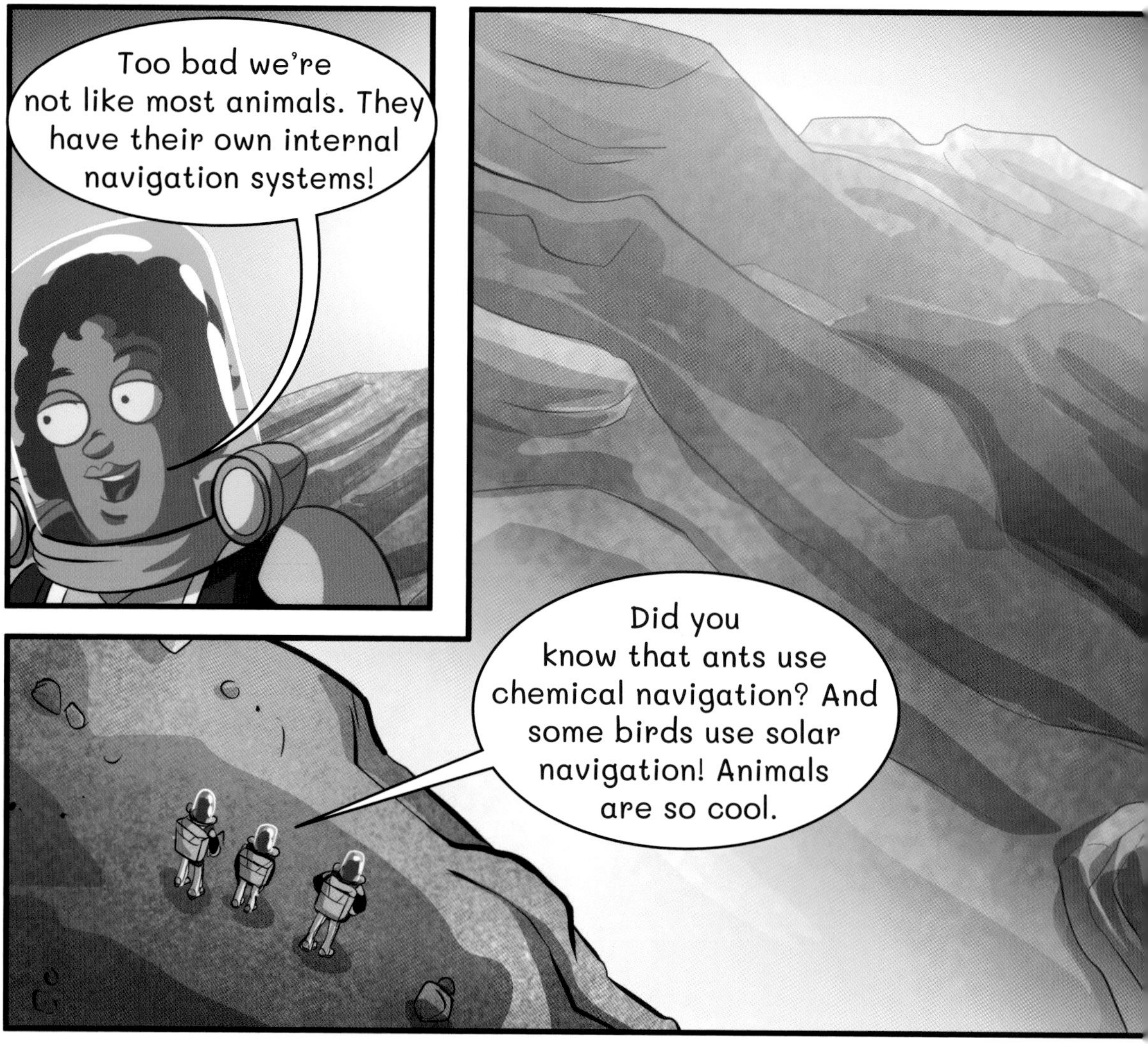
Too bad we're not like most animals. They have their own internal navigation systems!
Did you know that ants use chemical navigation? And some birds use solar navigation! Animals are so cool.

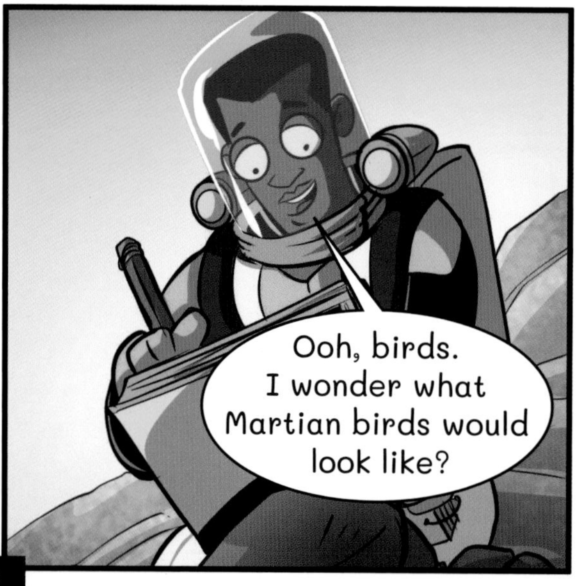
Ooh, birds. I wonder what Martian birds would look like?

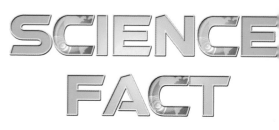

SCIENCE FACT

Birds called bar-tailed godwits fly from Alaska to New Zealand. This is the longest nonstop bird migration. takes about a week to complete. Th accomplish this by following the Sun.

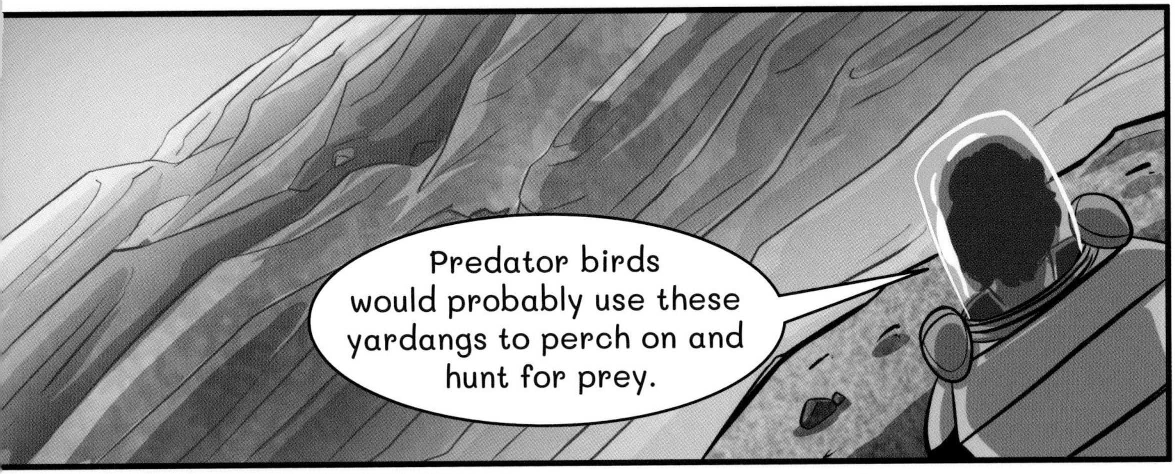
Predator birds would probably use these yardangs to perch on and hunt for prey.

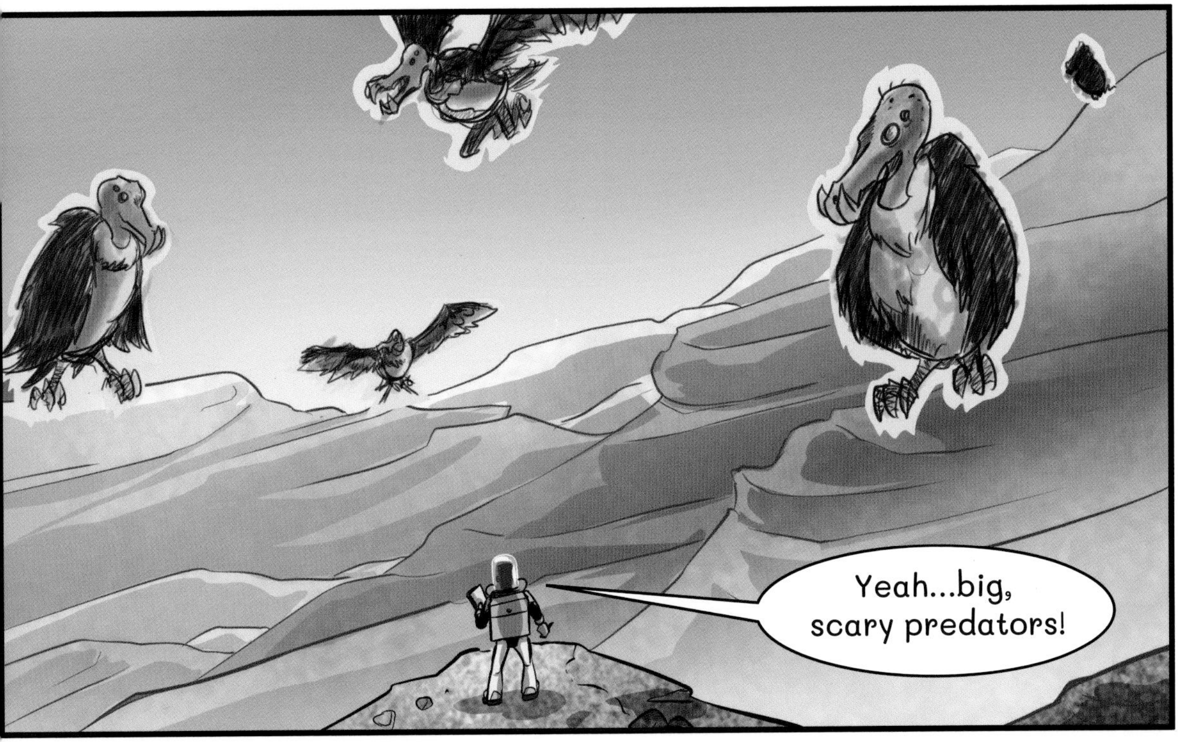
Yeah...big, scary predators!

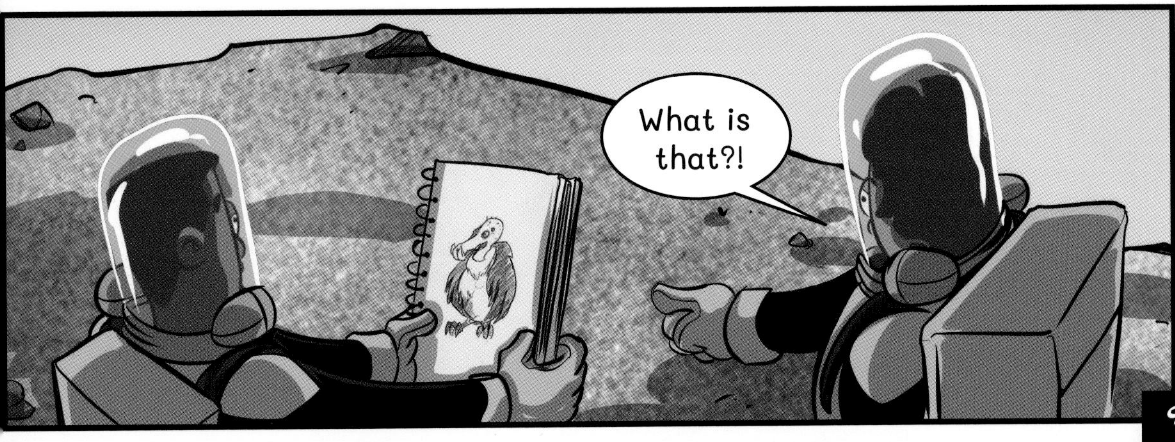
What is that?!

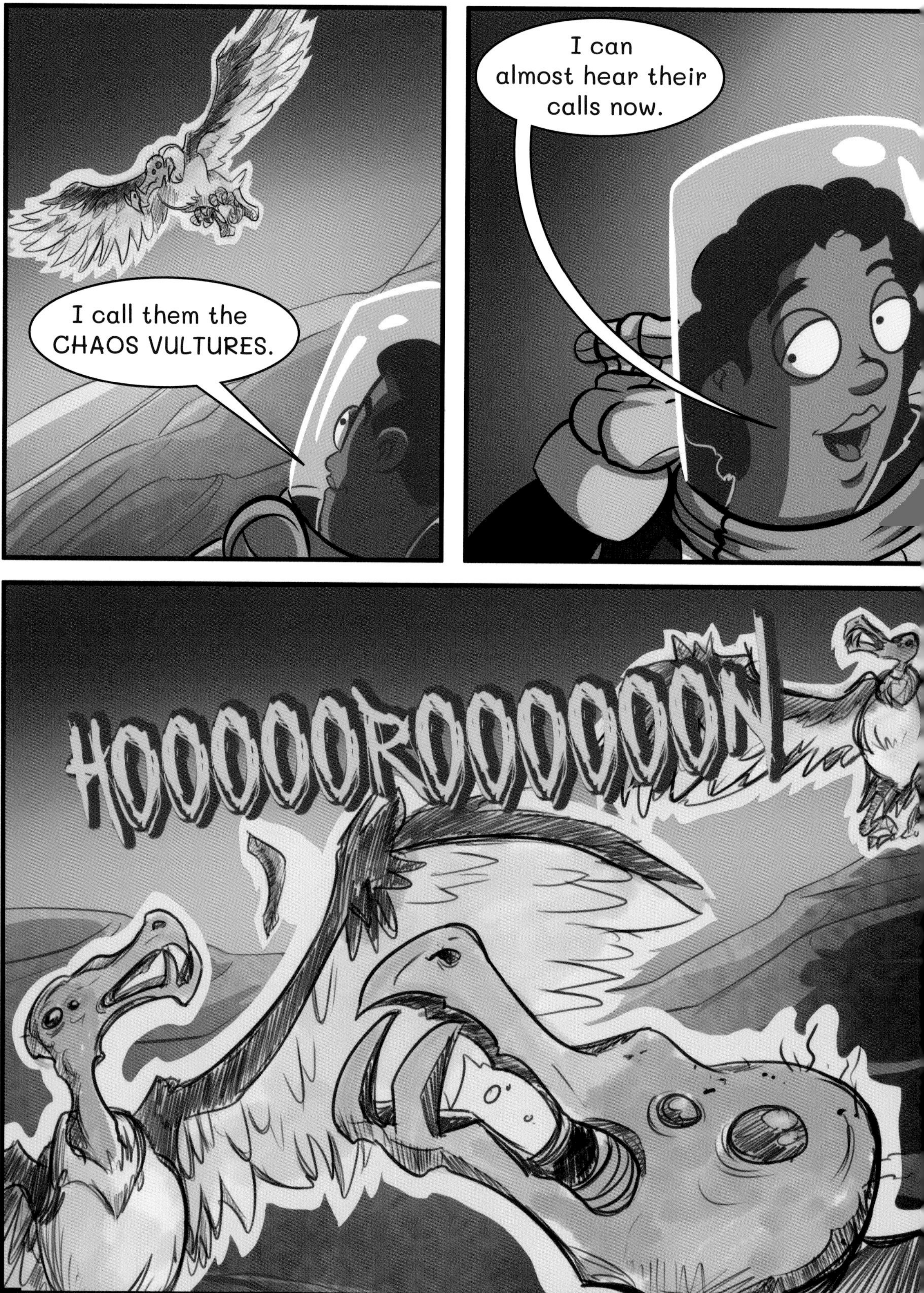
I call them the CHAOS VULTURES.
I can almost hear their calls now.
HOOOOOROOOOOOON

THE SCIENCE OF SCIENCE FICTION

The team talks a lot about navigation during this mission. On Earth, we use GPS to find our way. What exactly is GPS, and can it be used on Mars? Let's find out!

•GPS stands for Global Positioning System.

•It provides positioning, navigation, and timing, or PNT. On Earth, users can utilize PNT to get directions, calculate the distance of a run, or even play popular mobile games, like *Pokémon GO*.

•GPS is owned by the United States. There are 3 other similar global systems. They are operated by Russia, the European Union, and China.

•We need 3 things to use GPS: space, control stations, and users. Space is where satellites are placed. Control stations maintain the satellites. And users are us and the things we use that have GPS capabilities, such as smartphones and car navigation systems.

•As of 2021, the United States maintains 24 satellites for GPS. In total, there are 31 GPS satellites in orbit. The extra satellites are available to take the place of those in need of repairs.

•GPS receivers, like those in smartphones, measure the distance to each satellite. Satellites send signals to receivers. The receivers can tell where the satellites are by the amount of time it takes to receive the signal.

•GPS can also be used in space. Astronauts use it to track the large number of satellites circling the globe. Crewed missions use the guidance systems for missions closer to Earth's surface.

•Although GPS cannot be used in deep space like on Mars, NASA has developed a similar system. It can be used throughout the solar system. It is called the Deep-Space Positioning System, or DPS.

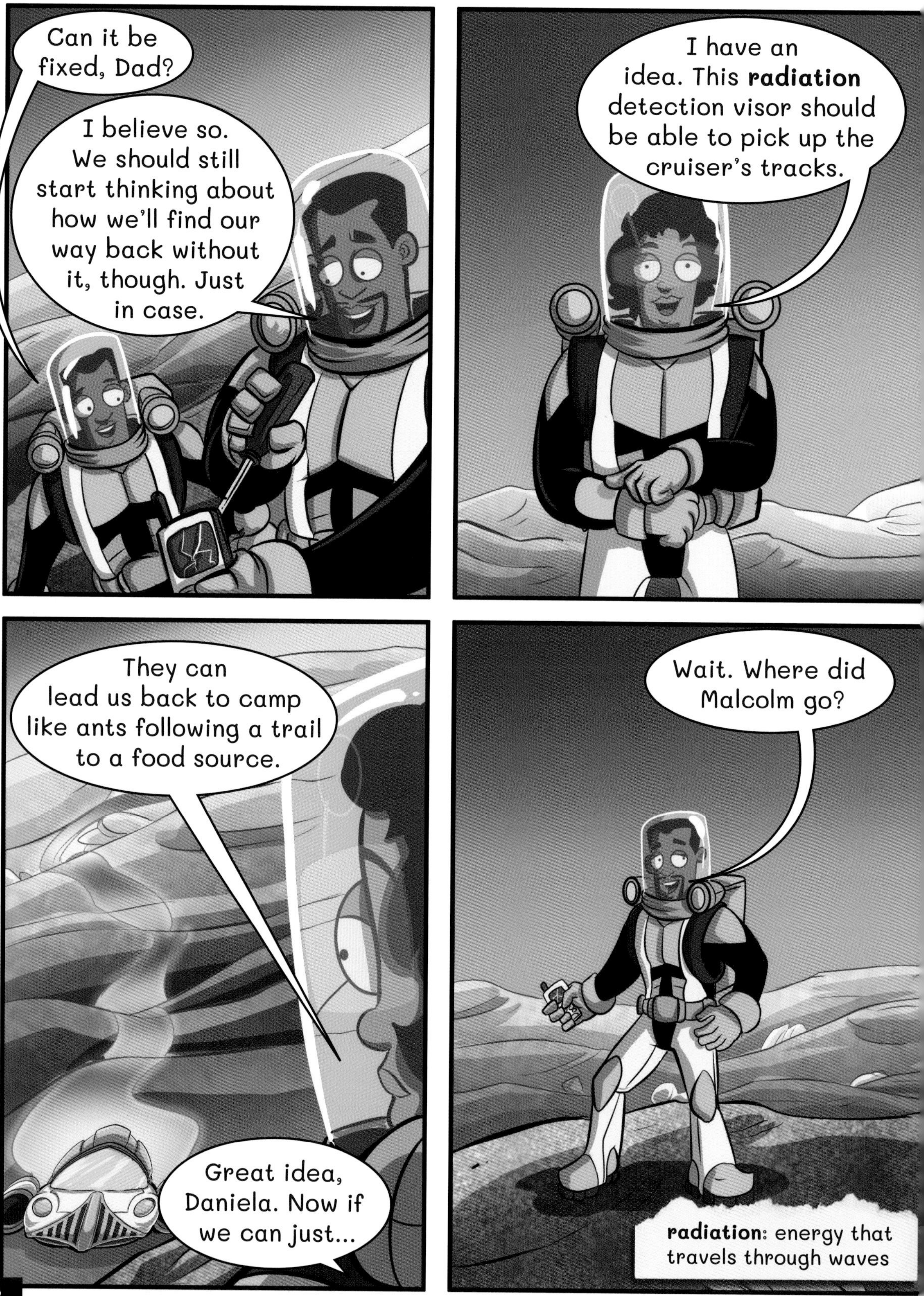
Can it be fixed, Dad?
I believe so. We should still start thinking about how we'll find our way back without it, though. Just in case.
I have an idea. This **radiation** detection visor should be able to pick up the cruiser's tracks.
They can lead us back to camp like ants following a trail to a food source.
Great idea, Daniela. Now if we can just...
Wait. Where did Malcolm go?
radiation: energy that travels through waves

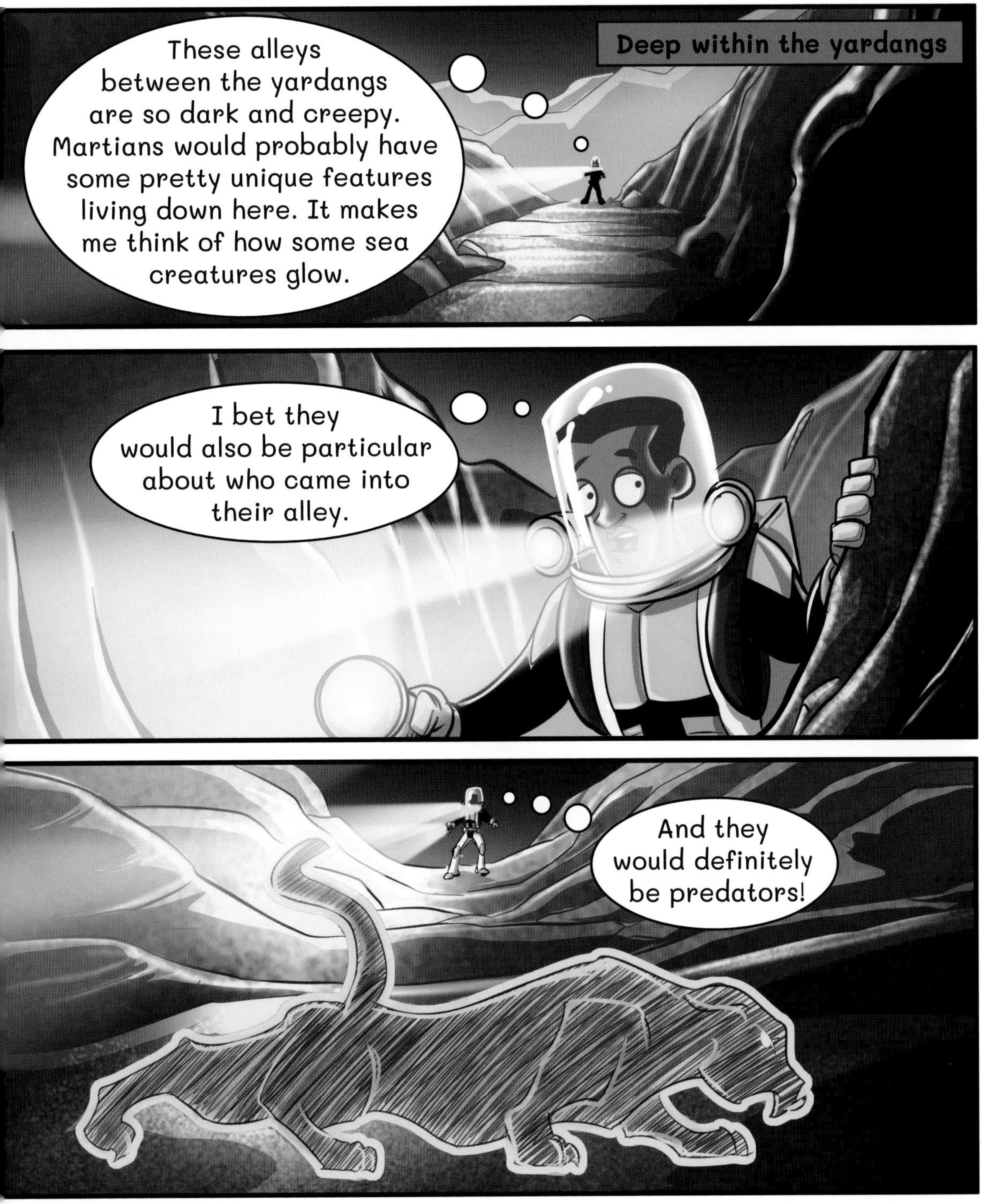
Deep within the yardangs
These alleys between the yardangs are so dark and creepy. Martians would probably have some pretty unique features living down here. It makes me think of how some sea creatures glow.
I bet they would also be particular about who came into their alley.
And they would definitely be predators!

SCIENCE FACT

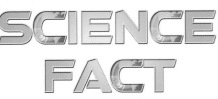

Predators are adapted to their environment. That means they are really good hunters where they live. An example is the cheetah, which has adapted to running faster than prey in the open grasslands of Africa.

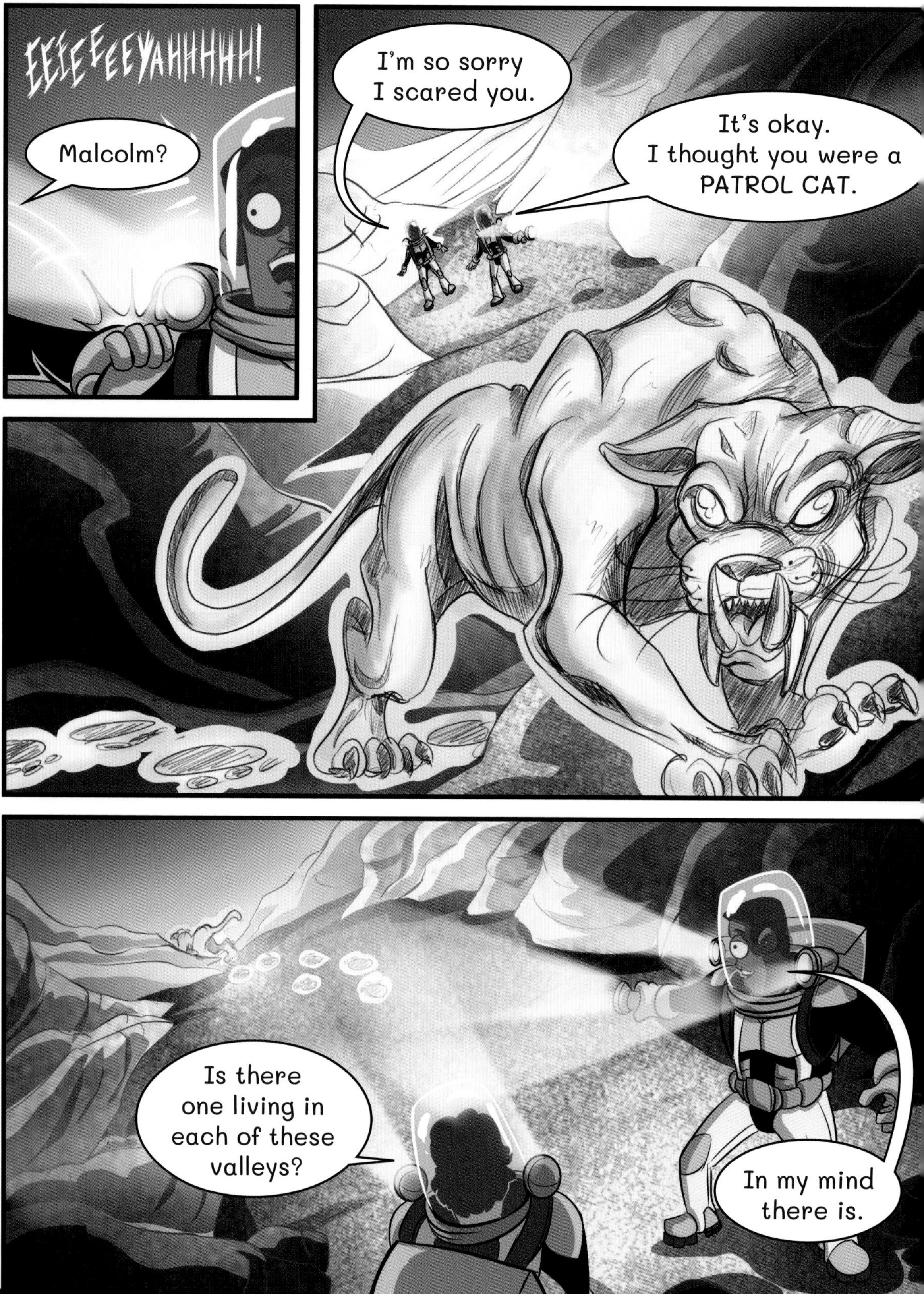
EEEEEEYAHHHHH!
Malcolm?
I'm so sorry I scared you.
It's okay. I thought you were a PATROL CAT.
Is there one living in each of these valleys?
In my mind there is.

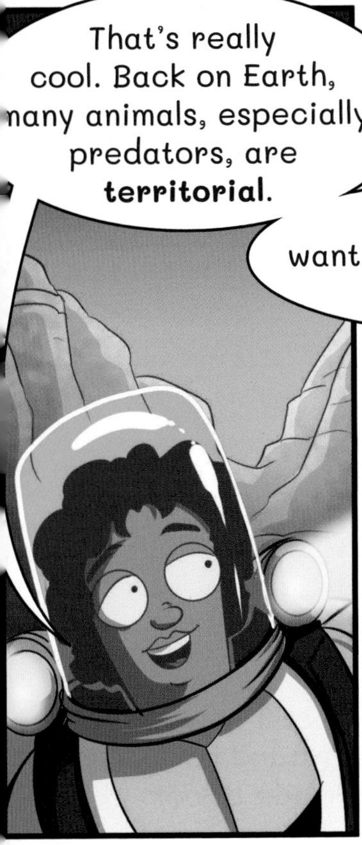
That's really cool. Back on Earth, many animals, especially predators, are **territorial**.
They don't want to have to compete for food.

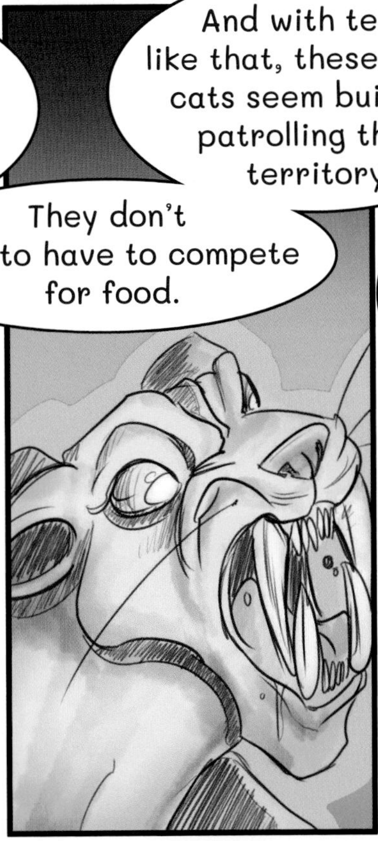
And with teeth like that, these patrol cats seem built for patrolling their territory.

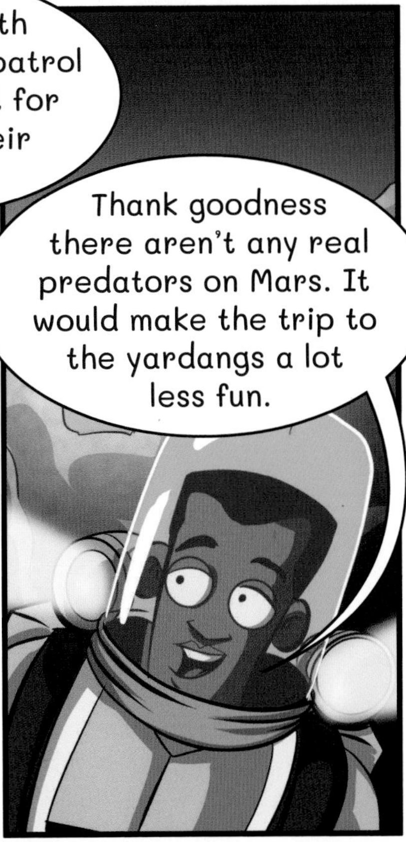
Thank goodness there aren't any real predators on Mars. It would make the trip to the yardangs a lot less fun.

SCIENCE FACT

ɔt all predators are g. On Earth they come all shapes and sizes. ıe Etruscan shrew is ırely 1.5 inches centimeters) long. But is a skilled hunter that ıts mostly insects ıd earthworms.

territorial: claiming areas of land as your own

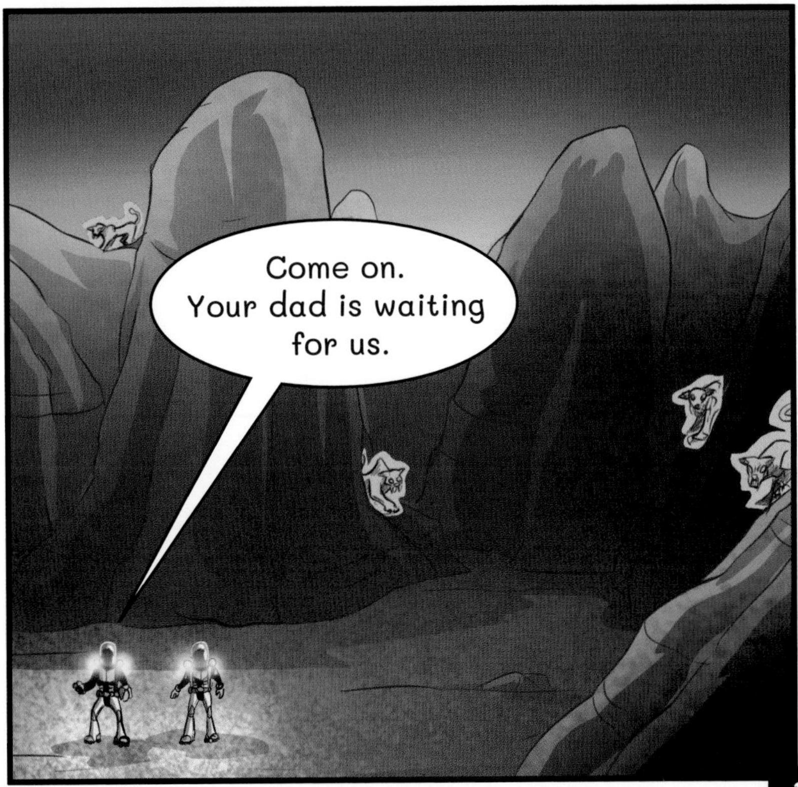
Come on. Your dad is waiting for us.

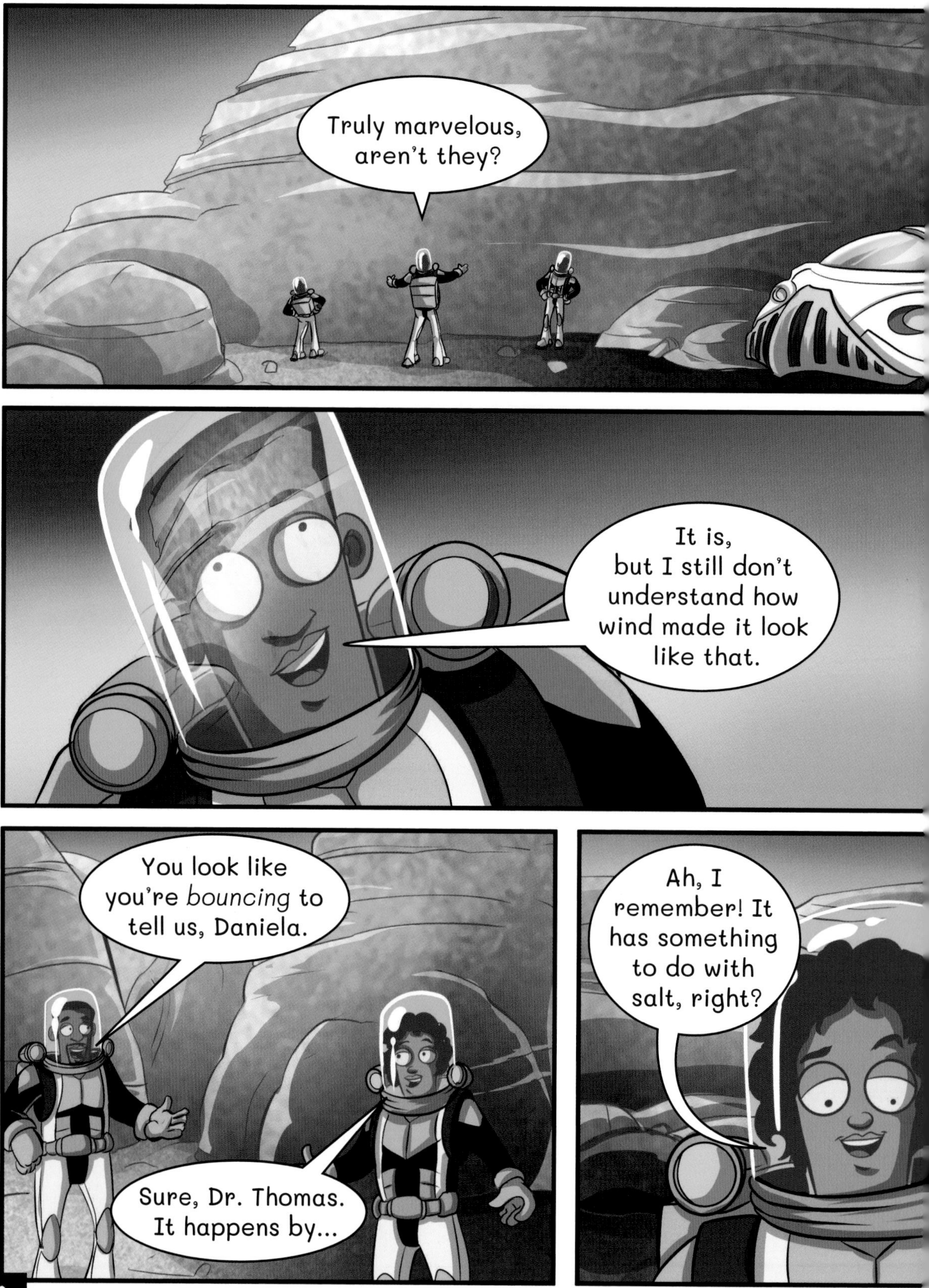
Truly marvelous, aren't they?
It is, but I still don't understand how wind made it look like that.
You look like you're *bouncing* to tell us, Daniela.
Sure, Dr. Thomas. It happens by...
Ah, I remember! It has something to do with salt, right?

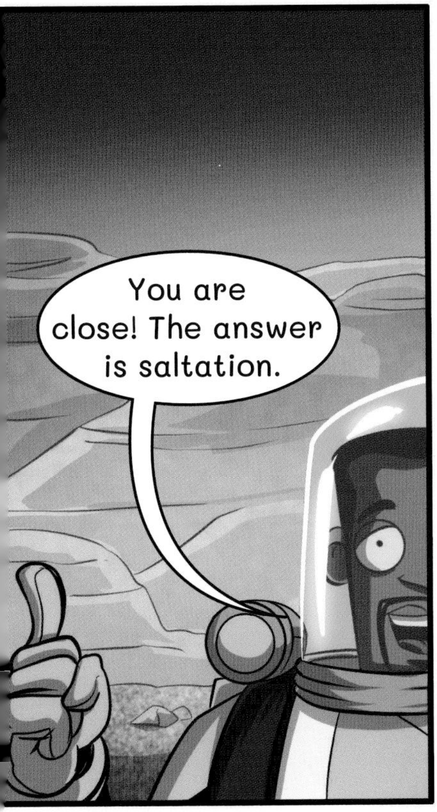
You are close! The answer is saltation.

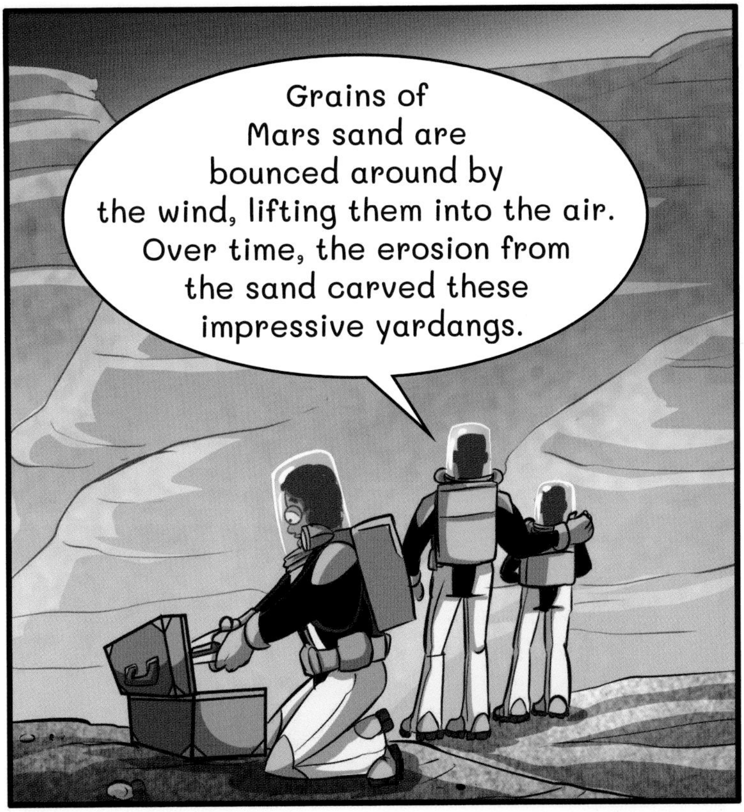
Grains of Mars sand are bounced around by the wind, lifting them into the air. Over time, the erosion from the sand carved these impressive yardangs.

MARS FACT

ı addition to yardangs, ıis region is also home ɔ **transverse** sand ridges. hey are small, crescent-haped formations that re found between the ardangs. Currently, cientists do not know ıuch about these ıysterious ridges.

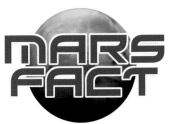

transverse: placed across something else

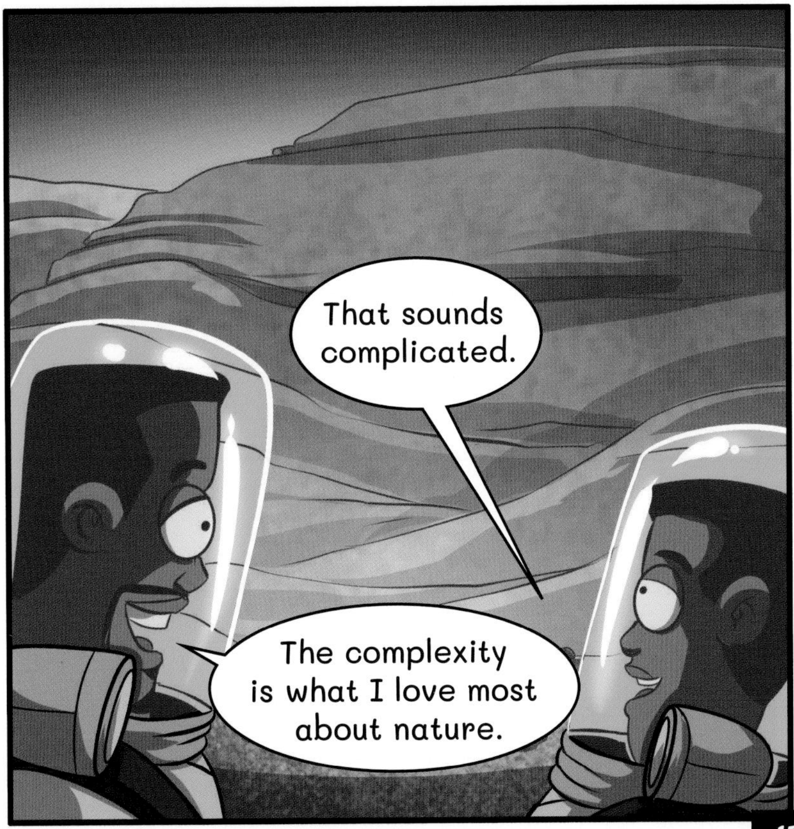
That sounds complicated.
The complexity is what I love most about nature.

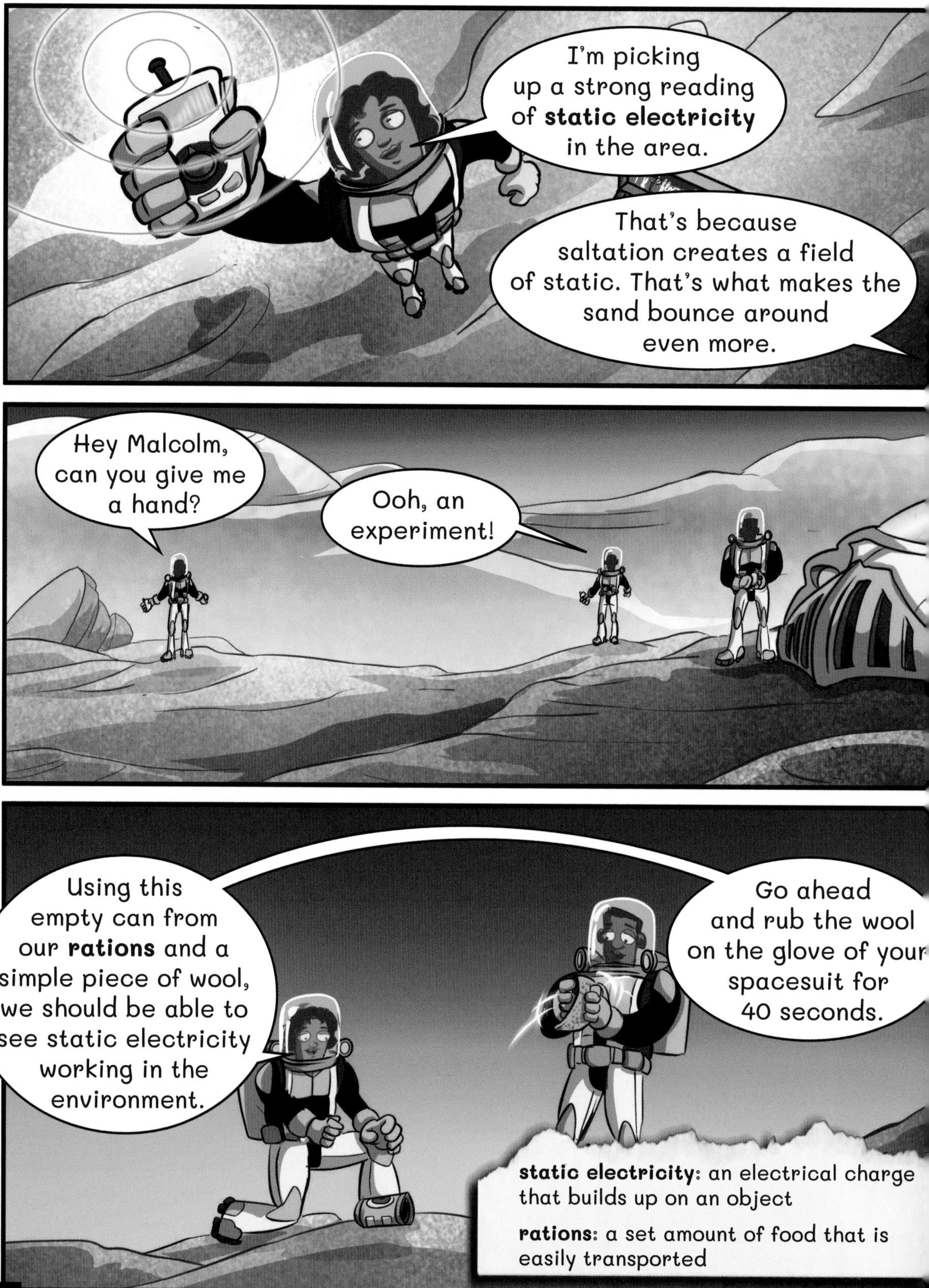
I'm picking up a strong reading of **static electricity** in the area.
That's because saltation creates a field of static. That's what makes the sand bounce around even more.
Hey Malcolm, can you give me a hand?
Ooh, an experiment!
Using this empty can from our **rations** and a simple piece of wool, we should be able to see static electricity working in the environment.
Go ahead and rub the wool on the glove of your spacesuit for 40 seconds.

static electricity: an electrical charge that builds up on an object

rations: a set amount of food that is easily transported

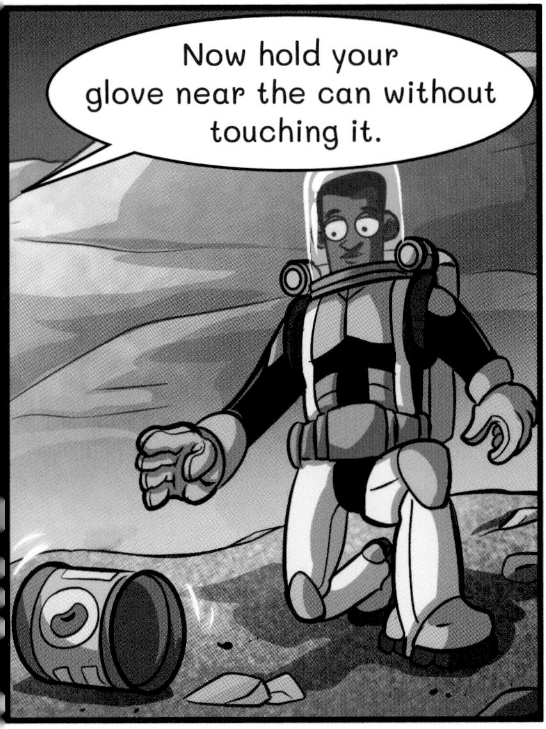
Now hold your glove near the can without touching it.

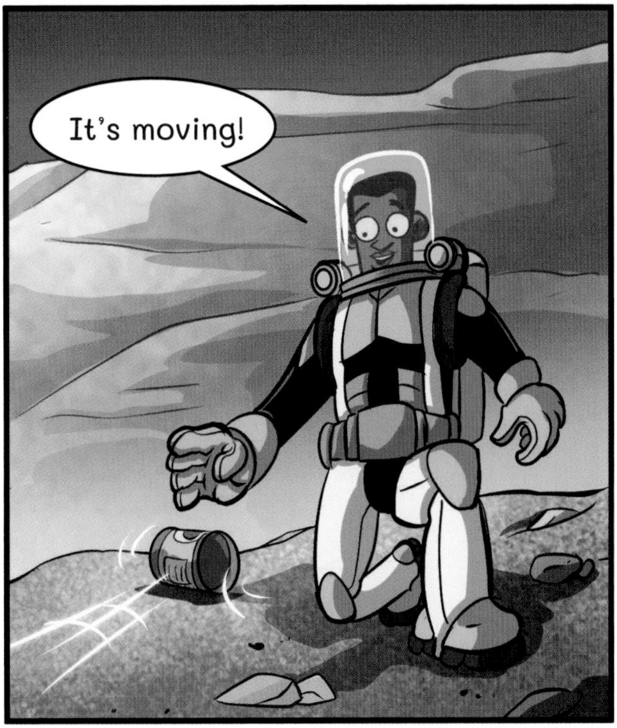
It's moving!

SCIENCE FACT

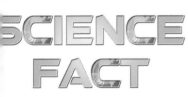

This is an experiment you can actually do at home. Don't worry though, you don't need a spacesuit! Just rub a balloon on your hair for 40 seconds. Then, hold the balloon near the can. Watch the can follow the balloon!

The movement happens because of static electricity. Rubbing the wool or the balloon causes friction, which charges the objects with static electricity. The wool and balloons have a negative charge. The can has a positive charge. The positive electrons are attracted to the negative electrons—and so the can will roll towards the balloon.

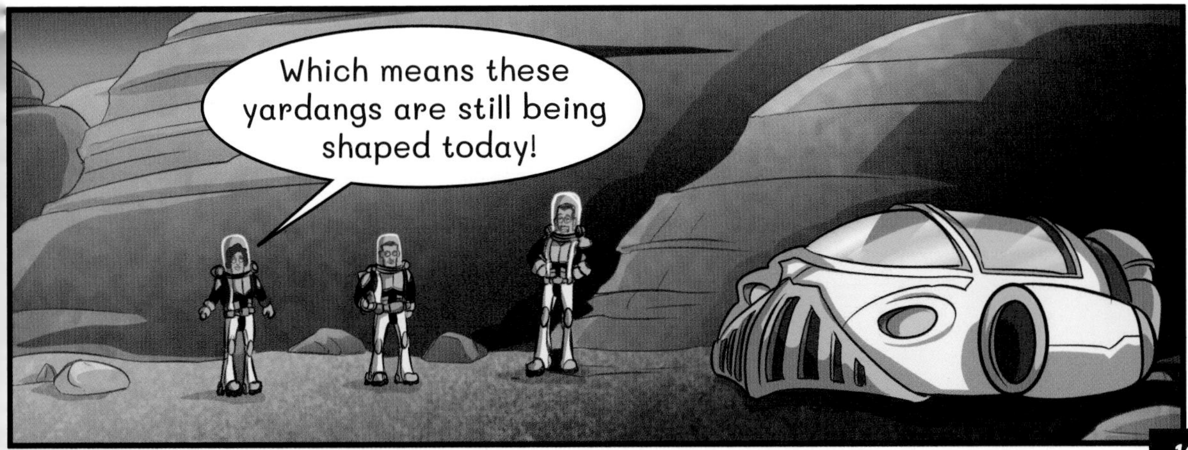
Which means these yardangs are still being shaped today!

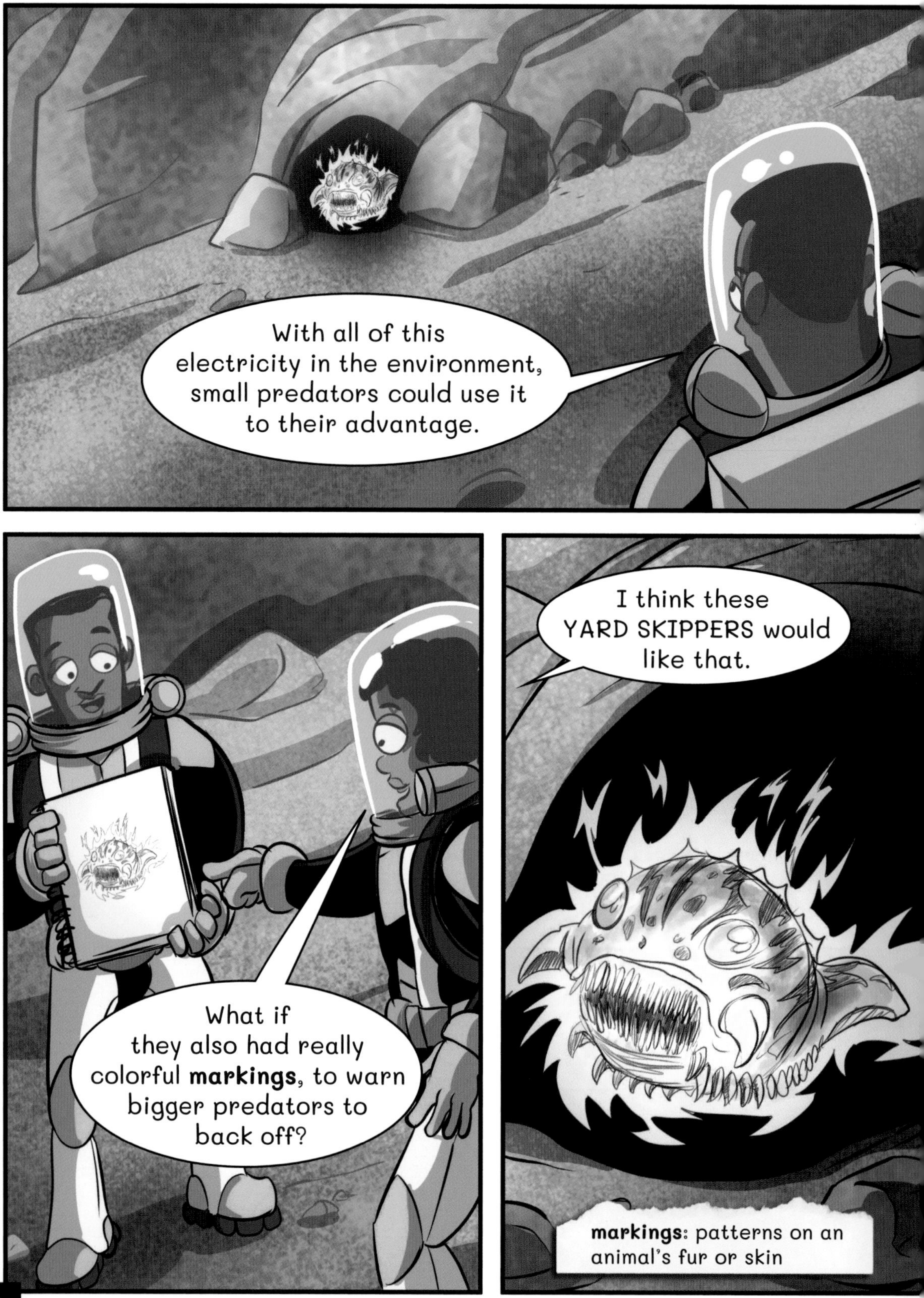
With all of this electricity in the environment, small predators could use it to their advantage.
What if they also had really colorful **markings**, to warn bigger predators to back off?
I think these YARD SKIPPERS would like that.
markings: patterns on an animal's fur or skin

THE FUNDAMENTALS OF ART

Let's put the FUN in the fundamentals of art by looking at the benefits of colors. Color can change the feeling of a drawing and the way people look at it.

• Warm colors like orange, red, and yellow suggest heat and excitement. They also appear closer in an image.

• Cool colors like blue, green, and purple suggest cold and calmness. They fade into the background of an image.

• Primary colors are red, yellow, and blue. All other colors come from these hues. A hue is a pure color that hasn't been mixed with other colors.

• Secondary colors are formed by mixing the primary colors together. For example, yellow and blue make green.

• Tertiary colors are formed by mixing primary colors with secondary colors. For example, the color aqua is a tertiary color. It is formed by mixing the primary color blue with the secondary color green.

ARTIST TIP: Warm and cool colors are opposite of each other on the color wheel. A color wheel is a chart used by artists to show the relationship between all colors. Try using a color wheel to help you make your creative choices. If the colors are close to each other on the wheel, they will be similar. Try using colors on opposite sides of the wheel to make your art really POP!

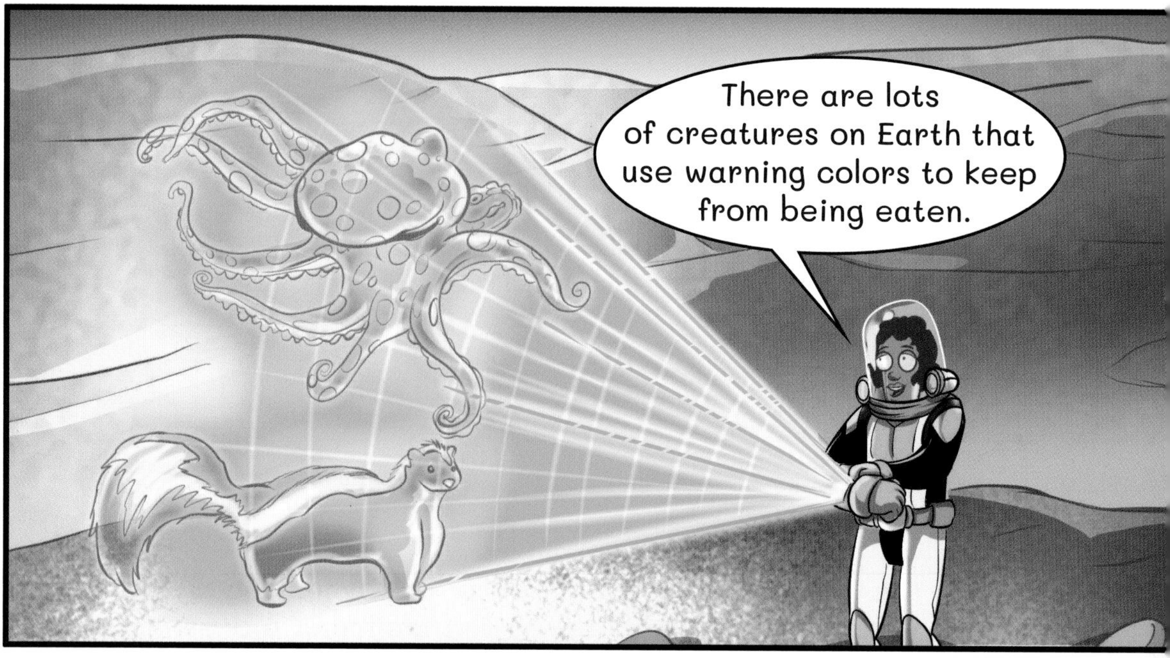
There are lots of creatures on Earth that use warning colors to keep from being eaten.

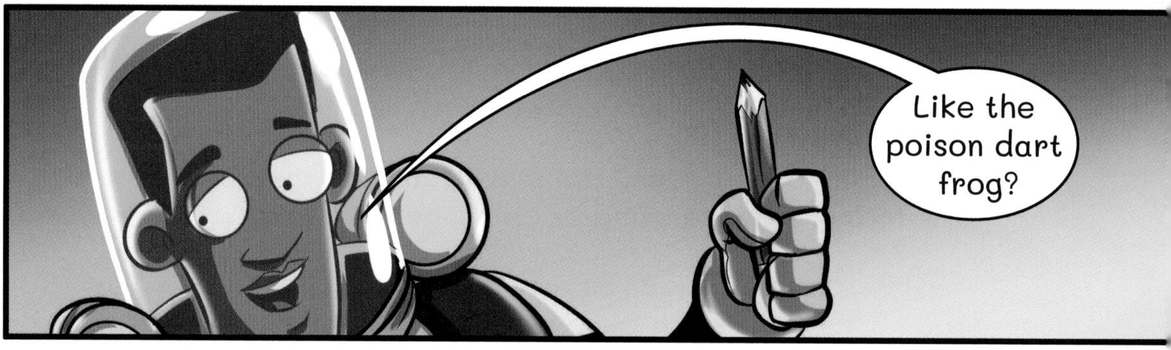
Like the poison dart frog?

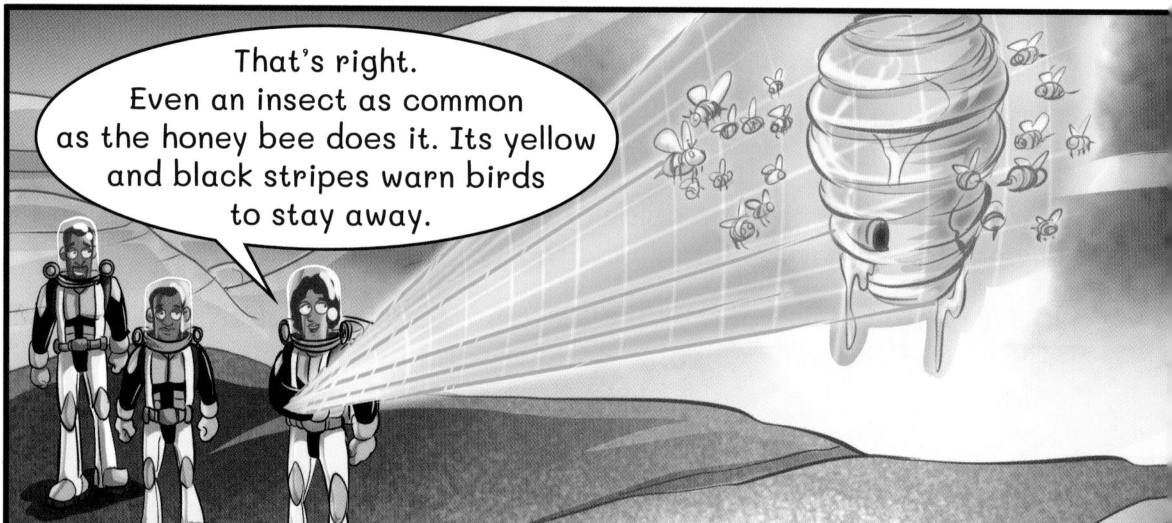
That's right. Even an insect as common as the honey bee does it. Its yellow and black stripes warn birds to stay away.

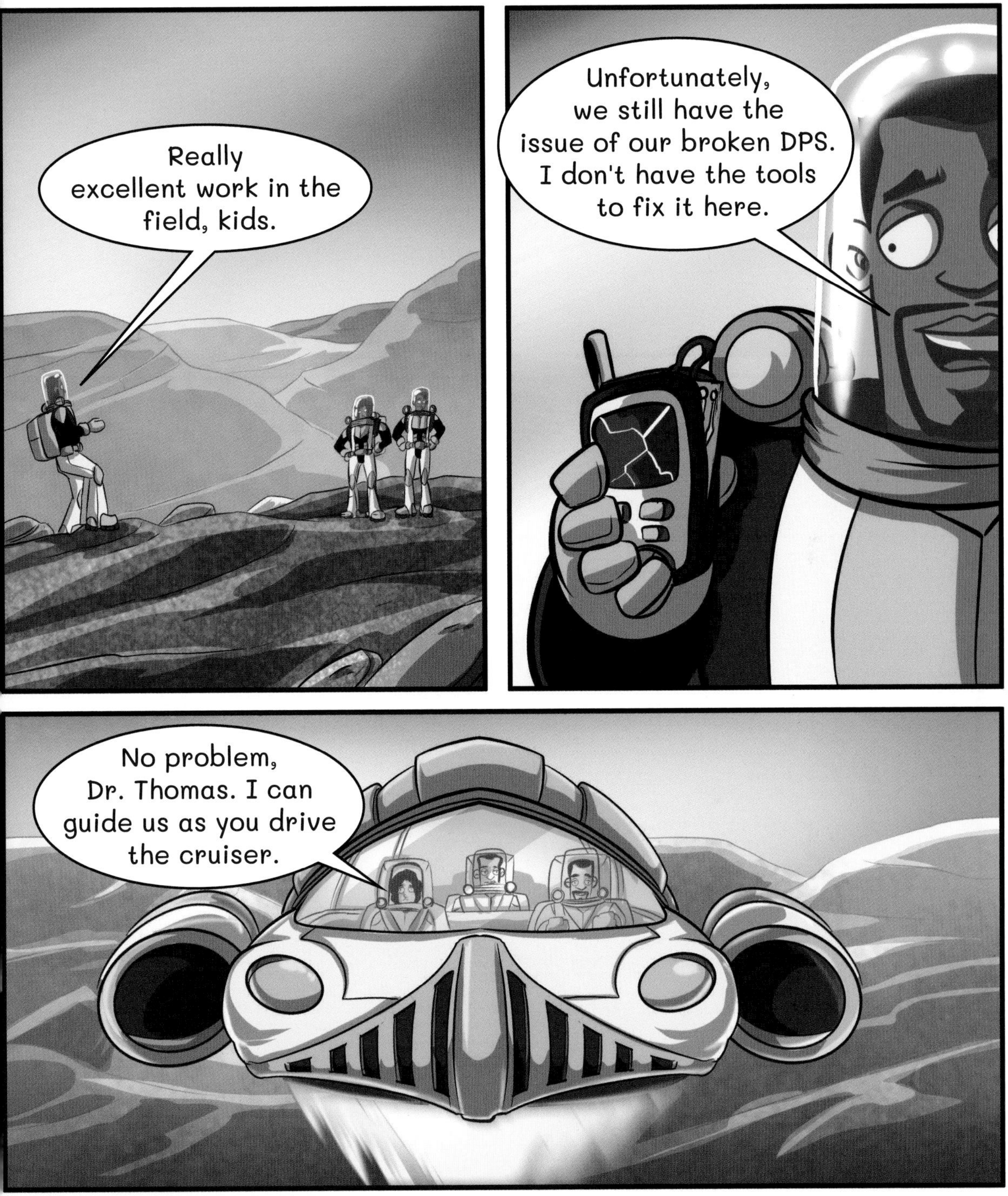
Really excellent work in the field, kids.
Unfortunately, we still have the issue of our broken DPS. I don't have the tools to fix it here.
No problem, Dr. Thomas. I can guide us as you drive the cruiser.

MARS FACT

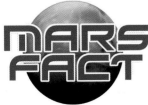

Mars rovers were built to travel only 110 yards (100 meters) per day. In 2015, the rover *Opportunity* completed its first marathon on Mars, having rolled 26.2 miles (42 kilometers). It took 11 years and 2 months to finish.

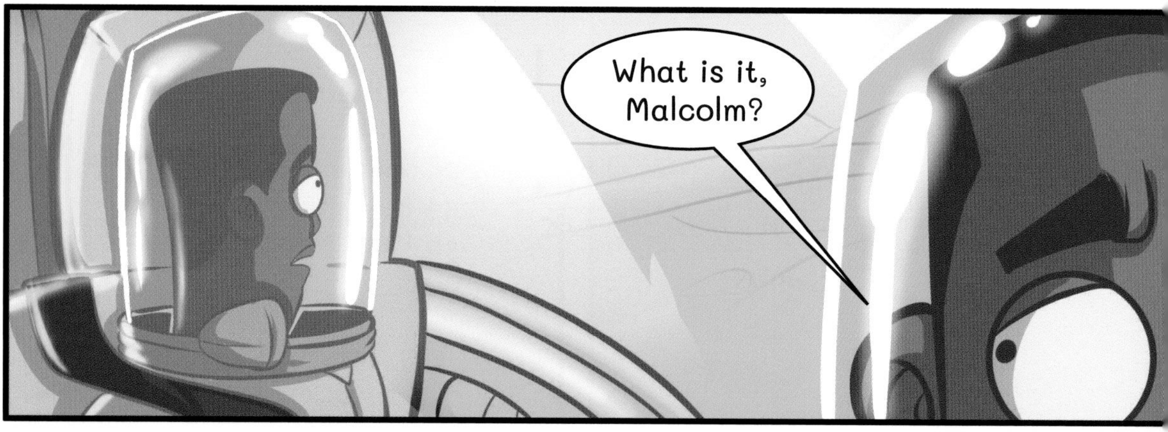
What is it, Malcolm?

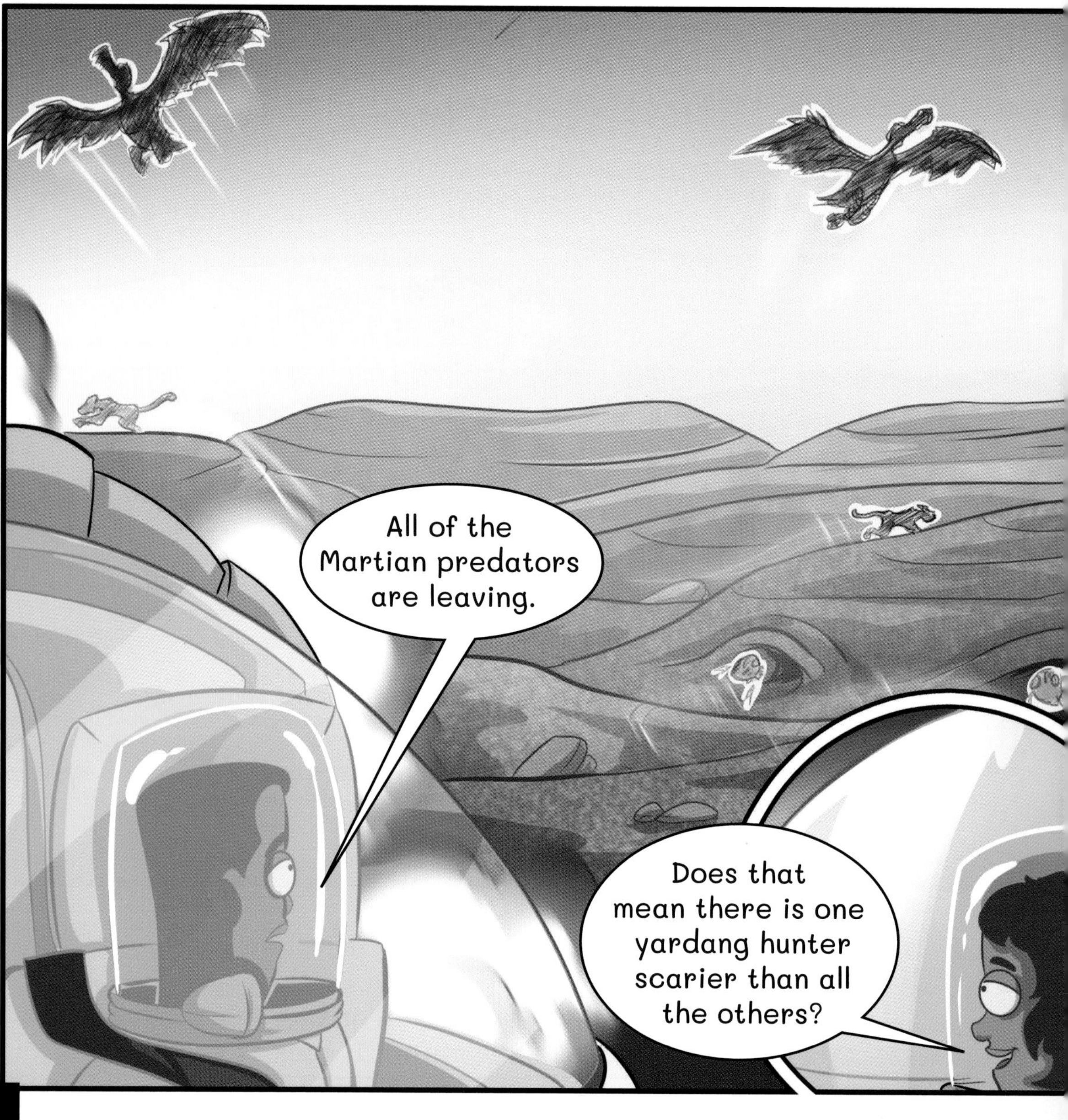
All of the Martian predators are leaving.
Does that mean there is one yardang hunter scarier than all the others?

MARS SURVIVAL TIPS

Whether you are camping in the wilderness on Earth or crossing an unfamiliar landscape on Mars, it is always smart to play it safe. Here are a few helpful tips on facing down a predator, no matter what planet you are on.

•Store your food in airtight containers to keep from luring predators into camp.

•Trash is just food you don't want anymore. Make sure it is properly stored as well.

•Never try to feed a predator.

•Know your surroundings. Knowledge of the area that you are in and the predators that live there will help you prepare.

•If you run into a predator, do not panic. Avoid **erratic** movement and make smart choices.

•Do not turn your back on a predator. This could cause them to attack.

•Remember, on Mars you are the real alien. Treat the planet with respect and be aware of your surroundings.

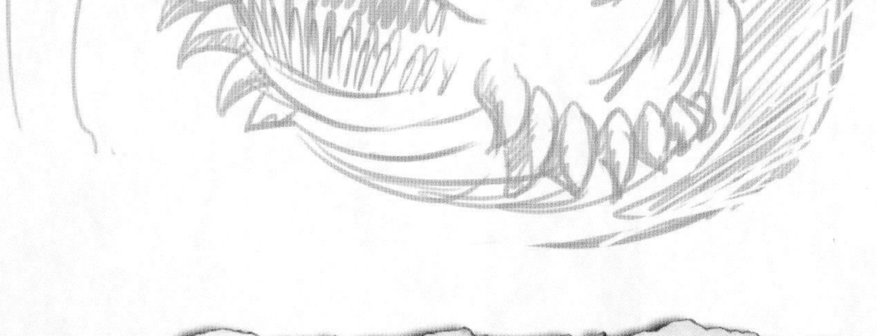

erratic: moving or behaving in an unpredictable way

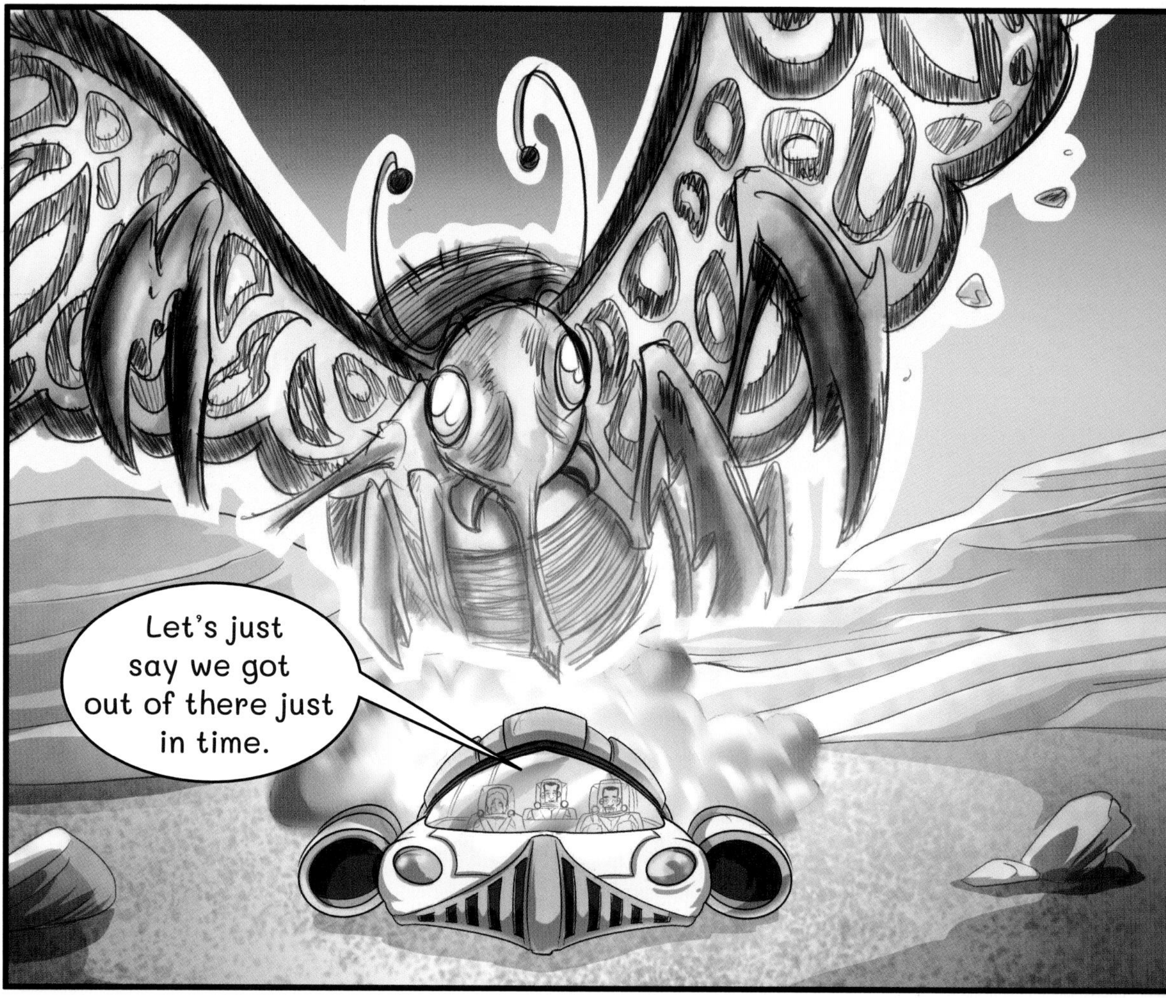
Let's just say we got out of there just in time.

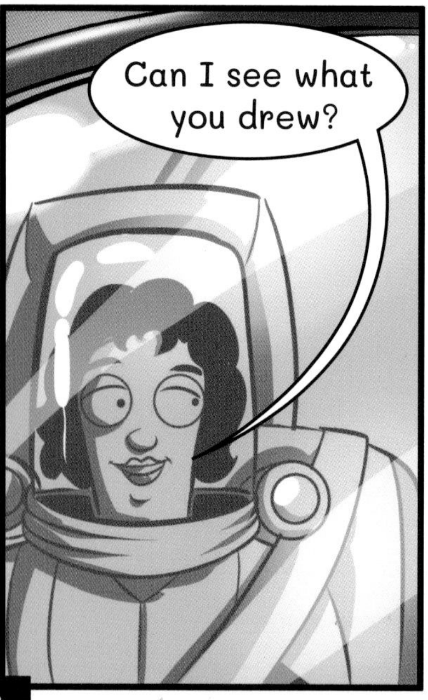
Can I see what you drew?

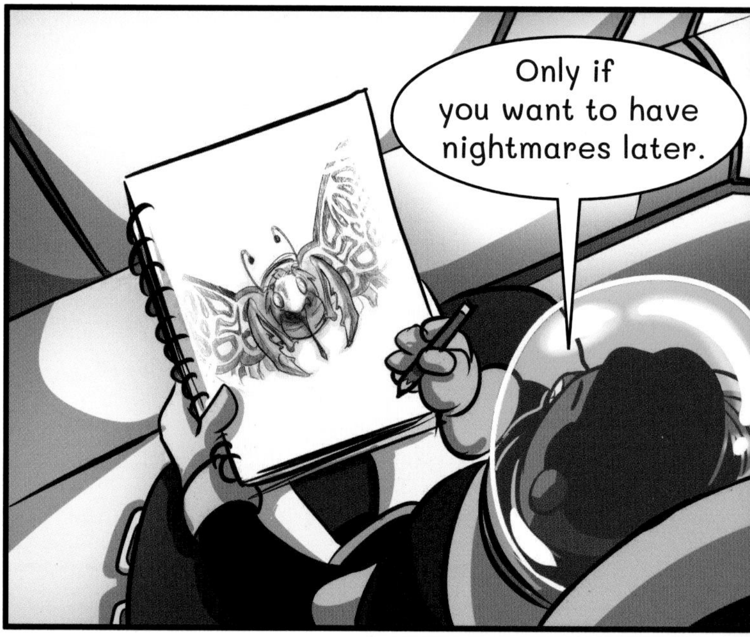
Only if you want to have nightmares later.

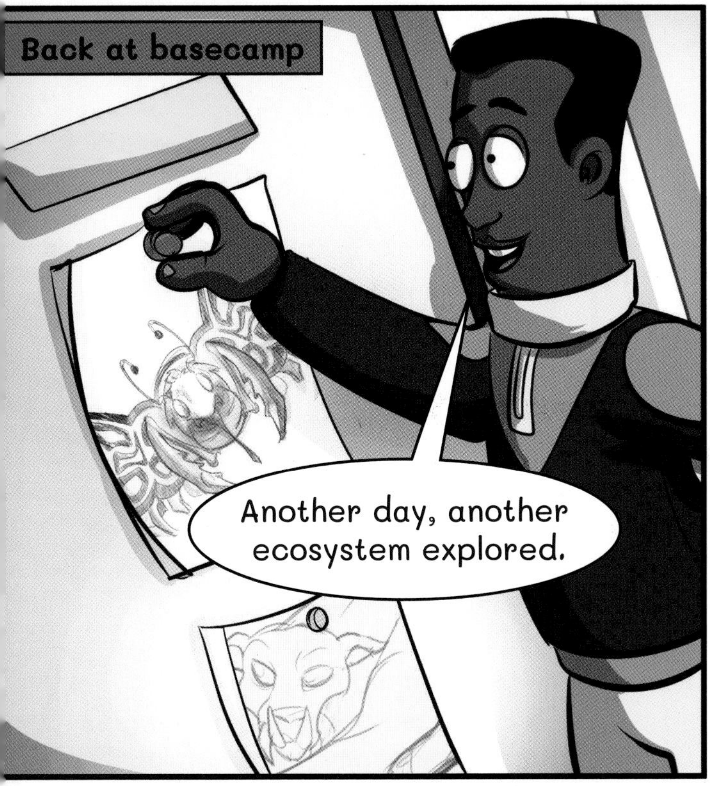
Back at basecamp
Another day, another ecosystem explored.

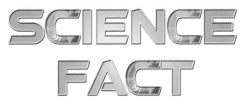

SCIENCE FACT

An ecosystem is a collection of all living and nonliving things in a particular place. Ecosystems are delicate. A change in temperature can impact the plants, which then impacts the animals who rely on them. Climate change, such as rising temperatures and changing weather patterns, is affecting many ecosystems on Earth.

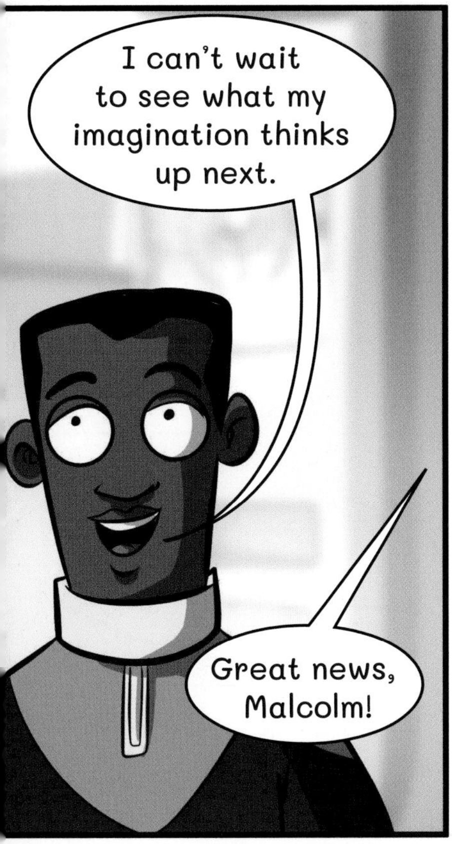
I can't wait to see what my imagination thinks up next.
Great news, Malcolm!

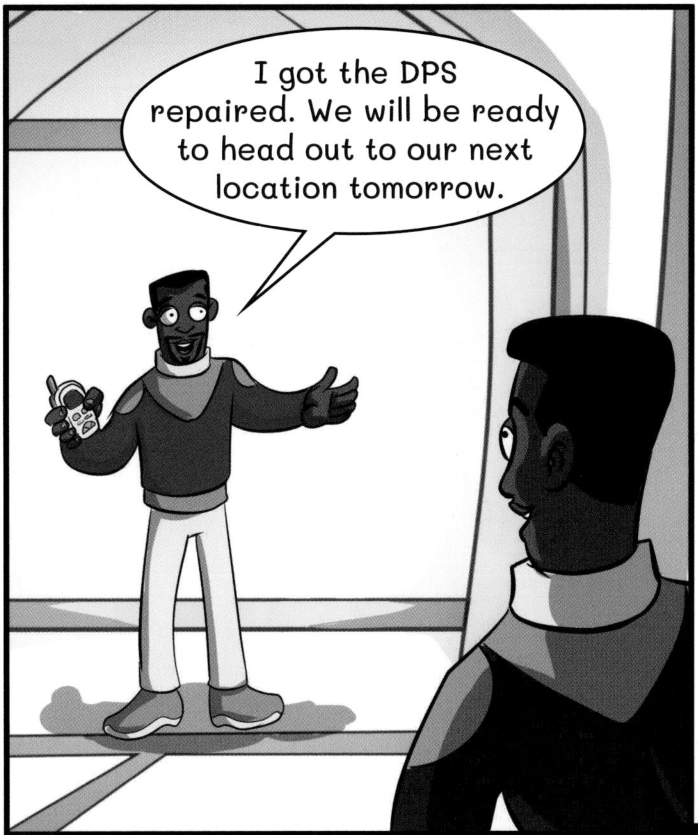
I got the DPS repaired. We will be ready to head out to our next location tomorrow.

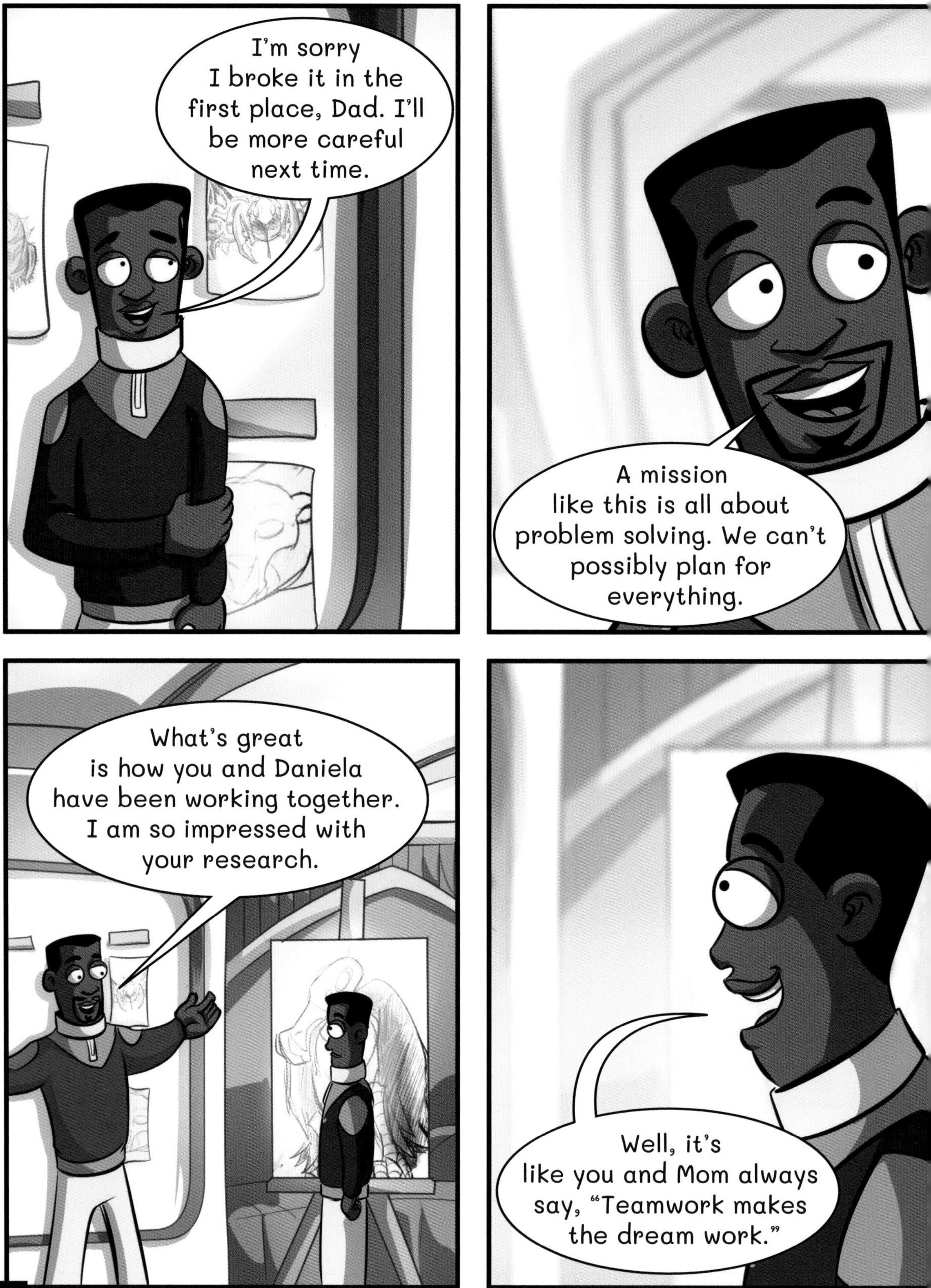
I'm sorry I broke it in the first place, Dad. I'll be more careful next time.
A mission like this is all about problem solving. We can't possibly plan for everything.
What's great is how you and Daniela have been working together. I am so impressed with your research.
Well, it's like you and Mom always say, "Teamwork makes the dream work."

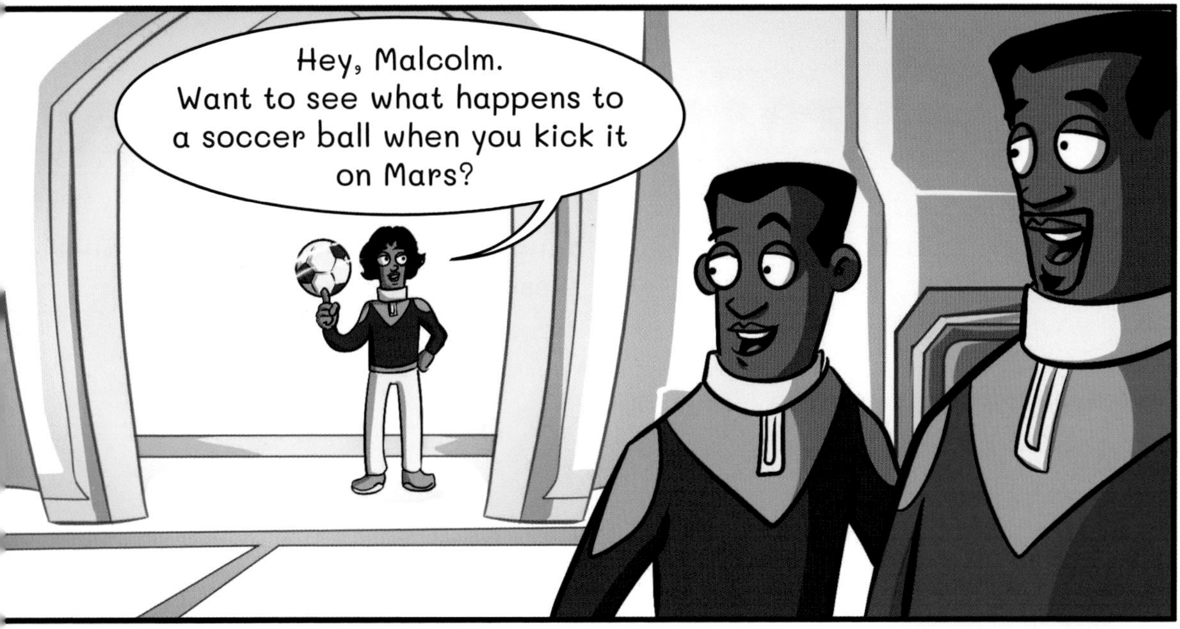
Hey, Malcolm.
Want to see what happens to a soccer ball when you kick it on Mars?

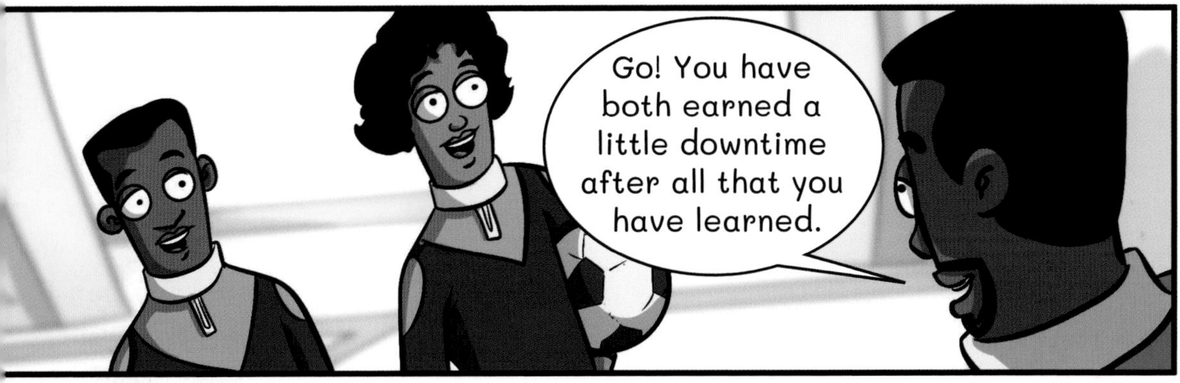
Go! You have both earned a little downtime after all that you have learned.

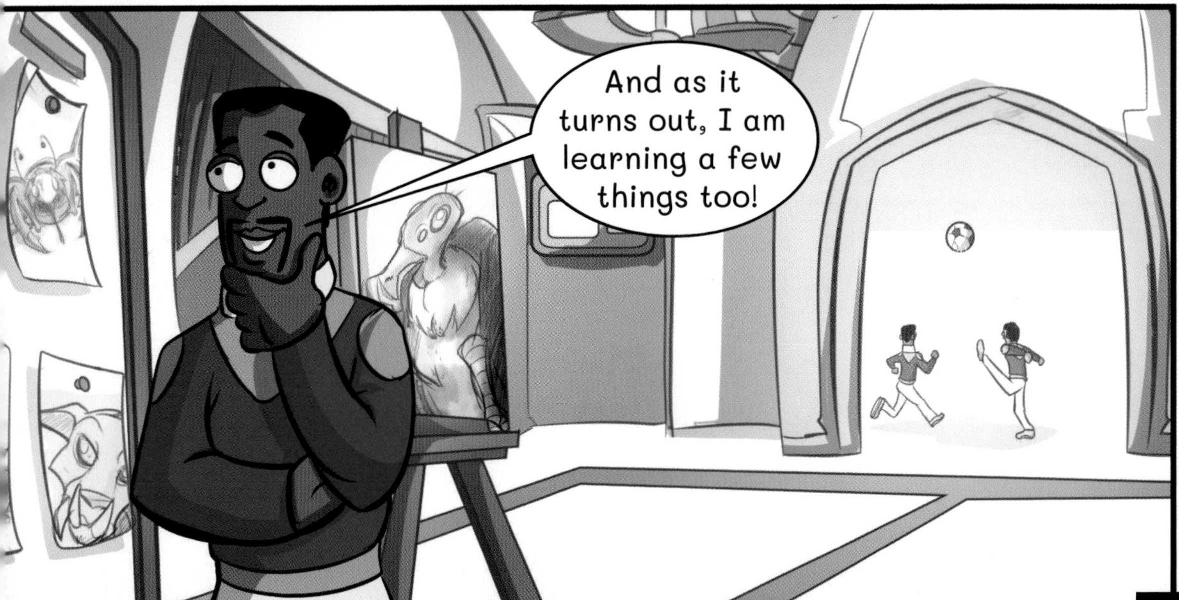
And as it turns out, I am learning a few things too!

HOMEMADE EROSION

Erosion helped to create the yardangs on Mars. You can mimic this natural process with just a few items that you can find around your home?

WHAT YOU NEED

• sand
• roasting pan that is at least 3 inches (7.62 cm) deep
• scissors
• paper cup
• water

STEPS TO TAKE

1. Pour the sand into the roasting pan. You may make a bit of a mess. Be sure to pick a place that is suitable for the experiment.

2. Make a slope in the sand by pushing more to one side of the pan tha the other. Don't be afraid to get your hands dirty. Have fun shaping "the land" with hills, mountains, and yardangs.

3. Have an adult poke a hole in the bottom of the paper cup with the scissors.

4. Hold the cup over the side of the pan with the most sand in it. Pour water into the cup. It will trickle out of the hole, over the sand, and travel to the other side of the pan. You will notice that it will take som of the sand with it. That's erosion!

SAFETY PAUSE

Scissors are sharp. Use only under adult supervision.

LEARN MORE

BOOKS

Bearce, Stephanie. *This or That Questions about Space: You Decide!* North Mankato, MN: Capstone Press, 2021.

Loh-Hagan, Virginia. *Mars Colonization.* Ann Arbor, MI: Cherry Lake Publishing, 2020.

WEBSITES

National Geographic: Planet Mars, Explained
https://www.nationalgeographic.com/science/article/mars-1

Learn about Earth's nearest neighbor and its mysteries.

Moving Around on Mars
https://mars.nasa.gov/mer/mission/timeline/surfaceops/navigation/

How do rovers move around on Mars? Read about how they explore, roll across the planet, and communicate with scientists on Earth

THE MARTIANS

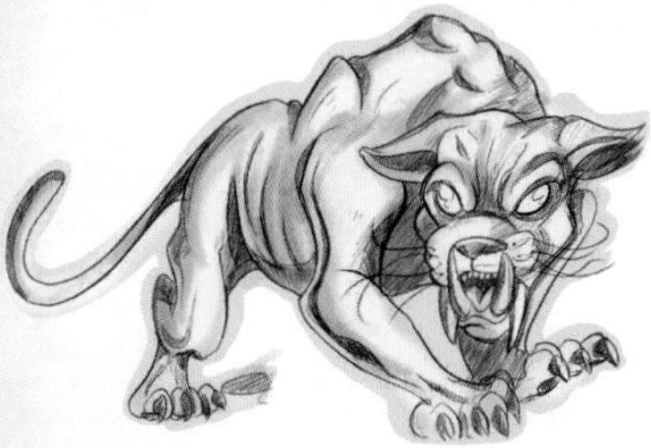

PATROL CATS

Solitary and territorial, Malcolm thinks up these glowing saber-toothed Martians to patrol the alleys that weave between Mars's yardangs.

CHAOS VULTURES

With trumpet-like beaks, Malcolm imagines that the blaring calls of these Martian birds of prey can be heard throughout the yardangs of Mars.

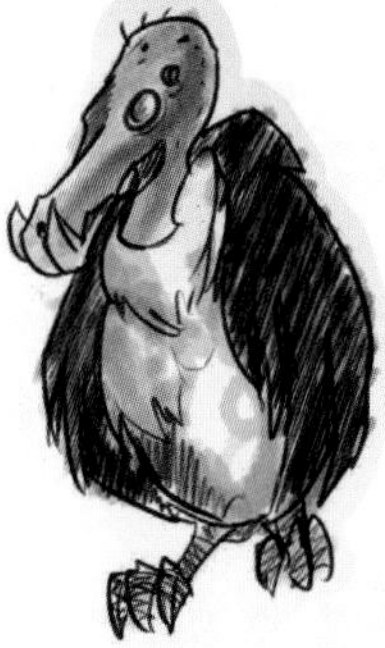

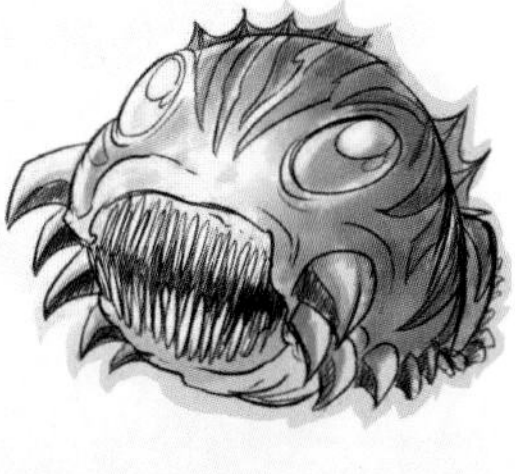

YARD SKIPPERS

Showing off mandibles that spark with electricity, these Martians resemble land-dwelling puffer fish. They are Malcolm's vision of the smaller predators of Mars.

GLOSSARY

canyon (KAN-yuhn) a deep valley formed by flowing water

chaos (KAY-ahs) without organization

craters (KRAY-tuhr) circular depressions in the ground

equator (EE-kway-tuhr) an imaginary line drawn around the middle of a planet that divides it in half

erosion (uh-ROW-shuhn) wearing away of land by nature

erratic (uh-RAT-tik) moving or behaving in an unpredictable way

formations (for-MAY-shuhn) objects, like rocks, with a formal structure

markings (MAR-kings) patterns on an animal's fur or skin

radiation (ray-dee-AY-shuhn) energy that travels through waves

rations (RAH-shuhns) a set amount of food that is easily transported

scaffolding (SKAF-uhl-dingh) temporary structure for reaching high areas

static electricity (STAH-tik ee-lek-TRIS-uh-tee) an electrical charge that builds up on an object

territorial (terr-uh-TOR-ee-uhl) claiming areas of land as your own

transverse (trans-VERS) placed across something else

yardangs (YAR-dahng) ridges formed by wind erosion

INDEX